# Conch Republic

## Vol. IV
## Dominica Dash

Look for other Western & Adventure novels by
# Eric H. Heisner

*Along to Presidio*

*West to Bravo (I)*

*Seven Fingers a' Brazos (II)*

*Above the Llano (III)*

*Del Río Hondo (IV)*

*T. H. Elkman*

*Mexico Sky*

*Short Western Tales: Friend of the Devil*

*Wings of the Pirate*

*Africa Tusk*

*Fire Angels*

*Cicada*

*Citation for Murder*

*Flight of the Windigo*

*Conch Republic, Island Stepping with Hemingway*

*Conch Republic – vol. 2, Errol Flynn's Treasure*

*Conch Republic – vol. 3, Coba Libre*

Follow book releases and film productions at:
www.leandogproductions.com

# Conch Republic
## Vol. IV
## Dominica Dash

## Eric H. Heisner

Illustrations by
### Emily Jean Mitchell

Visit our website at
www.leandogproductions.com


Illustrations by: Emily Jean Mitchell
Contact: mlemitche@gmail.com
Website: www.mlemitchellart.com


Dustcover jacket design: Dreamscape Cover Designs


Edited by: Story Perfect Editing Services – Tim Haughian

Paperback ISBN: 978-1-956417-38-8

# Dedication

The memory of J.B. – life lessons learned, and an inspiration through his music & philosophy.

# Special Thanks

Amber Word Heisner, Emily Jean Mitchell

## Note from Author

My friends often tease me that my family vacations and travels are just excuses for me to come up with writing ideas. They're not wrong... Getting out of the normal routine opens my mind to all sorts of exciting scenarios and adventures. Western author, Louis L'Amour, often said that he had been to every location he wrote about. With excursions to Mexico, Jamaica, Dominica (sounds like: daa ·muh ·nee ·kuh), and the Florida Keys, I've walked the ground (and took the boat ride!) of many of the places I write about.

Come along on another island adventure, as the routine in Key West doesn't keep our writer in one place for long. Every storyteller knows that to keep the well from going dry, new experiences, good and bad, need to come into the mix. Even when you're writing in paradise...

*Eric H. Heisner*

April 21st, 2025

# I

$A$ new day breaks over the Florida Keys. At the end of the road on the island of Key West, birds chirp, as a gentle breeze rustles through swaying palms. Following the off-season weeknight events, there is a serene peacefulness in the air. Despite its earned reputation as a spirited party town, the main thoroughfare of Duval Street has the sleepy feel of a remote island getaway.

Bobbing its head as it trots across the street, a feral chicken stops to peck at something on the ground before turning and moving on. Far off, the rattling clank of a bicycle chain can be heard, as a two-wheeled cruiser makes its way across town. A lively pair of Common Grackles dart from perch to perch, leapfrogging their way down the empty sidewalk.

In a small, carriage-house apartment located on an old historic Key West estate, adventure author Jonathan

# Eric H. Heisner

T. Springer (alias, *J. T. Springs)* sits typing away on his laptop computer. Noticing daylight, he looks up to the window and peers out at the tropical garden. Then, he sits back in his chair and stretches.

Turning back to his illuminated computer screen, he sighs with satisfaction at the amount of work completed. "That's enough writing for now... I wonder what the *rest* of the world is up to."

Jon condenses his page of writing and opens his email. He scans the messages and notices one from the PR department of his California literary agent, C. Moselly. When he clicks on the email, a message pops on screen.

*Exclusive Book Premiere & Party Extravaganza for mystery/adventure novelist, J. T. Springs' newest release: "Coba Libre – Treasure of the Mexican Jungle".*

Snorting with amusement, Jon looks away from his computer to his travel bag across the room. Propped-up in the corner, the crumpled backpack sits empty and deflated. Turning back to the email invitation, he slowly scrolls down. "Party extravaganza, huh...? Can't wait to see what the final artwork for the cover looks like."

The new book's dust-jacket displays a jungle-motif adventure theme with an *Indiana Jones* type hero, pistol in hand, saving a dark-haired, tanned, bikini-clad woman. Behind them is a small lagoon with a monstrous crocodile, mouth open wide. Jon laughs at the misleading image and continues to scroll down to read the rest of the message.

# Dominica Dash

*We cordially invite you to attend the*
*book release event for your exciting new novel,*
*"Coba Libre", at the exclusive Capitol Resort in*
*Mexico City. Please respond with the number*
*of guests you will be attending with.   - C. Moselly*

Jon sighs and shakes his head as he continues to scroll down the page to preview the new volume's back cover layout. A Mayan temple in the jungle is overlayed with a review from a literary magazine, a few celebrity blurbs, and a story synopsis. He smiles when he sees the author bio has no photo attached. "Slim chance of getting me *anywhere* near *that* silly circus." Selecting the rsvp button on the invitation, Jon types a reply.

*Dear Moselly,*
*Book cover looks exciting.*
*Thanks for getting another one published.*
*No, I will not be attending the event.*
*Sincerely,*
*JTS*

Jon stretches his arms over his head and gazes out the window again. Relaxing, he glances at the Evite on the laptop. Then, he clicks away from the page and closes his email. Considering his writing progress so far, he then looks over at the kitchen table and a note written on Conch Republic Tavern stationery.

# Eric H. Heisner

*Congratulations Jon! So excited to hear that your first book is due to be published soon. Let me know when it comes out, and we'll have a release party at the Conch Tavern.*

*Your friend,*
*Angie*

He looks at a slender hardcover novel with a simple cloth cover and gold leaf stamped title: *The Island of Haves & Have-nots, by Jonathan Tyler Springer*

Reaching across the table to pick up his author's copy, Jon examines the spine and flips the book over to open the back. On the last page, he sees his Hemingway-esque author photo and a short bio: *Jonathan Tyler Springer is a traveler & writer based in Key West, Florida. This is his first novel.*

Putting the hardcover aside near Angie's note, Jon closes the screen on his laptop. Turning to the view out the window, he sees storm clouds coming in and then looks over at the empty travel bag. Getting up from his chair, he grabs a set of socks and running shoes from the hallway and sits on the couch to put them on.

After tying them, Jon stretches and heads for the door. Just as he steps outside, a drop of rain splats on his forehead. He moves back inside right as the heavy downpour begins. With sunlight still shining through the pouring rain, he watches the droplets splash at his feet for a moment before deciding that it isn't the best time for a jog.

Taking a seat back on the couch, he looks around the small apartment and thinks about his plans for the day. Outside, the rain continues, so he lays down and closes his eyes. The pattering sound of rainfall on the carriage-house's metal roof is like melodic drumming. Relaxing to the soothing sound, Jon is asleep in no time.

# II

A high-winged seaplane, with a Key West Air Charters logo painted across the fuselage, races through the sky, darting around patches of storm clouds. Jon, sitting in the copilot seat, looks over at Rollie behind the controls. He notices the pilot's intense sense of urgency as the pop of gunfire is heard and a bullet skims the windscreen, cracking the glass.

"What the hell..." Jon leans forward to peer out the port window and sees two Russian-make jets with Cuban markings. "Rollie, we got two fighters at nine o'clock!"

"I see 'em..." The pilot pushes on the yoke and the seaplane dives toward the choppy waters below.

The rivets of the vintage airframe rattle with the sudden increase of speed, and Jon blurts, "You plan to outrun them?"

# Dominica Dash

As the jets zoom past, Rollie flashes a grin, pulls out of the dive and reaches up to ease back the overhead throttles.

"Bingo…"

While the pair of military aircraft tilt their wings to bank and come around, Rollie scans the dark horizon and replies, "We ain't gonna outrun a pair of MiGs in this old goose."

As the seaplane levels out at approximately one hundred feet altitude, Rollie keenly studies the expanse of open ocean below. From the copilot seat, Jon cranes his neck to locate the fighter jets. "What's your plan then?"

"We're going to make it very difficult for them."

As the MiGs come around again at their six o'clock, urgent radio chatter breaks through. Jon adjusts his headset and quizzically looks at Rollie. "My little bit of Spanish is rusty. What did they say?"

"Nothing all that interesting…" Rollie clicks the radio off and hooks a thumb toward the cargo hold, directing Jon to go. "Git back there and break open one of those weapon crates. Lock and load, point it out the starboard hatch and give 'em somethin' to think about."

Jon stares at the pilot in disbelief, until Rollie gives him a serious look and urgently tilts his head toward the back. Reluctantly, Jon unbuckles his seatbelt to comply, muttering, "Rollie, I really don't think this is a good idea."

"Add it to the list. You should have spoken up before you agreed to come along."

"You said this was going to be a milk run!"

"It usually is…"

# Eric H. Heisner

Squeezing past the pilot, Jon heads toward the back of the plane. Strapped to the floor of the cargo hold are several wooden boxes with foreign markings stenciled on their sides. Jon breaks into a sweat, feeling nauseous as he studies the symbols depicting guns and ammunition from the Cold War. "This is *not* a good plan." Then, poking his head back into the cockpit, he asks, "Which ones do I open?"

Brusquely sliding back his headset from over one ear, the pilot turns to Jon. "For now, I'd leave the bazookas alone and go for the AKs."

Jon does a shocked double-take to the crates of munitions and states, "Everything is written in *Chinese!*"

Another popping round of gunfire from the MiGs turns Rollie's attention back to the controls. Baffled, he glances over his shoulder to Jon. "Hell, *I* can't read that language, *either.* Assume the big ones are rocket launchers, medium for rifles, and the smalls are probably ammunition."

Studying the stack of wooden boxes, Jon now notices the differing sizes. Reluctantly, he heads back into the cargo hold and starts to unfasten the tie-down straps. Then, using the claw end of a hammer, he pries open one of the medium sized boxes. A nervous chill sweeps over him, as he looks inside to see a row of surplus military machine guns. "*Why* am I *doing* this?"

Dragging a small box closer, he opens it to find banana clips of ammo inside. He takes a magazine out, pulls a gun from the crate and slaps the stick of ammunition into the receiver. Then, when the seaplane jolts violently, Jon drops the loaded weapon and tumbles over the stack of crates. From the cockpit, Rollie hollers an apology, which Jon can barely hear over the roar of the radial engines.

On his feet again, Jon picks the weapon up and moves toward the starboard hatch. He unlatches the panel and, with a burst of stormy air, it swings open. As a torrent of moist, tropical air washes past him, he tries to locate the position of the fighters in the dark sky. His gaze then drifts to the churning waters a hundred feet below. Grabbing a headset and plugging it into the intercom, Jon adjusts the microphone and speaks. "Hey, Rollie… What am I supposed to do back here?"

A voice responds, "Shoot at those bastards!"

"Where are they?"

"I don't see 'em."

"I don't, either!"

"Well, they didn't give up and go home."

"On the bright side, they're not shooting at us anymore." Wind whipping his hair back, Jon sticks his head outside and spots the pair of fighters coming around again to track their flight path. Suddenly, he sees the flares from a round of tracers, as the Cubans open fire.

A stream of bullets rip past them, some of them hitting their mark, while others spatter into the choppy ocean below. Over the intercom, Rollie hollers, *"Shoot back, dammit!"*

Jon examines the foreign weapon, then cradles the military machine gun under his arm and pulls back the bolt. Unsure of himself, he stutters into the headset. "Uhhh, Rollie… I… I don't think I know how to use this particular firearm."

"Just *shoot* the *damn thing!!!*"

Jon points the barrel outside and squeezes the trigger. The weapon spews brass shell casings, as gunfire erupts from its muzzle. Aiming the automatic rifle as best he can, Jon squeezes off another burst of bullets, as the jets fly by and then circle around for another pass.

Clicking the trigger to find the gun empty, Jon looks back to the box of ammunition. Ejecting the hollow banana clip, he grabs a loaded one and fits it into the receiver of the gun. Outside, the fighters are returning, and Jon yells over the intercom. "Dammit, Rollie...! This is *absurd!!*" On the horizon, heavy clouds indicate that a squall is forming, and the seaplane banks low toward the looming storm, as the MiGs prepare for another fly-by. Jon leans out to see where they are and observes the menacing skies ahead. "Why are we flying into the storm?"

The intercom crackles. "With your bad marksmanship, we'll need *some* kind of cover."

Lowing his weapon, Jon peers out at the dark, swirling clouds ahead. "We can't fly into *that!*"

"Right... Neither can *they!*"

Jon pokes the gun out the hatch again, pulls back the bolt and returns fire as the Cuban fighters buzz past them. He ceases firing and hollers into the intercom. "Next time, remind me not to ever go on these trips with you again..."

The intercom crackles, breaking Rollie's voice up. "Why...? This has been great research for your writing."

Wind and rain swirl in through the open hatch, as the plane flies into the storm. Raindrops splash against

Jon's face, and he looks at the machine gun in his hands. He turns to the crates of contraband in the cargo hold, then back out to the military jets that are bearing down on them. Shaking his head, Jon tries to wake from this terrible dream. "Mosely, I don't want to write these stories anymore…"

Suddenly, there is a loud *bang*, and Jon's eyes pop open. Wiping beads of moisture from his face, he looks to the screen door of the apartment, as it idly swings closed after a strong gust of wind passes through. The door swings open again, and mists of rainwater blow in.

Unsettled, Jon sits up and stares outside at the dark, tropical storm. Not yet fully awake, he gets up, closes the door and then sits back down on the couch. He thinks about Rollie, the seaplane and their imagined Cuban encounter, and he eventually clears the vision from his overactive imagination. "Sometimes, I don't know if I'm awake or dreaming…"

Resting his head against the wall, he wipes the rain from his face and takes a deep, calming breath.

# III

The storm has passed, leaving a glistening layer of wetness on everything and lengthy channels of wet debris along the curbs. Jon jogs on the empty sidewalk, avoiding the deeper puddles. Following his usual route down Duval Street, he turns past the Hemingway house, continues on toward mile-marker 0, and then runs east toward the public beaches.

After the heavy rainfall, the streets are mostly vacant and there is an overwhelming sense of loneliness on the island. Up ahead, a Key West Police vehicle lingers at an intersection. As Jon trots by, he looks to see if he can recognize the officer inside, but only vaguely makes out the hand on the steering wheel waving back at him. Jon returns the greeting and continues to jog homeward.

The skies are still grey and cloudy, when Jon walks up the metal stairway to the living space above the carriage-house. Half-expecting some sort of surprise visitor, he scans his apartment, but all is quiet. After removing his sweated t-shirt, he heads to the bathroom, muttering, "Nothing going on here... I wonder who's down at the Conch Tavern."

~*~

Dressed in a pair of khaki shorts and a casual button-down tropical shirt, Jon walks to the Conch Republic Tavern. Passing the Clipped Kitty, he notices a shadowy figure pass by one of the windows. Seeing a curtain flutter, he stops to stare, but quickly realizes that he must look a bit creepy standing there staring at a house of ill-repute. His gaze moves to the empty street, and then he glances back once more before walking away.

As he steps inside the tavern, Jon sees that it, too, is nearly empty. He goes to the bar, sits at his regular stool, and waits for the bar's owner, Angie. Instead, an older woman emerging from a back-room heads over to greet him.

Flora Blanca is a well-traveled woman in her mid-sixties who obviously maintains an outdoor lifestyle. Set against a row of perfectly white teeth, her deeply-tanned skin looks like a protective leathery shell. "Hey, muchacho... What's doin'?"

Jon snaps into a vivid flashback of his recent Mexican adventure with Rollie, but quickly shakes it off. As she stops opposite him on the other side of the bar, he smiles at her. "Hello, Flora. Where's Angie?"

The mature woman grins and offers him a sly wink. "She's with Rollie on a work trip around the Lesser Antilles. Said she'd be gone at least a week."

# Dominica Dash

Jon can't help but feel a bit disappointed when he thinks about her note mentioning the party for his new book release. As he realizes that two of his very few friends on the island are gone for a good while, a sense of loneliness washes over him. "When did they leave?"

"Yesterday morning… When you didn't stop by the night before, Angie mentioned I should care for you while she was gone. Want the usual?"

Jon gives a nod, and Flora grabs a glass and turns to the beer tappers. While quietly humming a tune under her breath, she pours him a Sunset Ale. Pivoting on his stool, Jon gazes around the quiet barroom. In a corner booth, a group of local fishermen chat over drinks and, at another table, an older tourist couple peruses a guidebook for sight-seeing options on a rainy day. As Flora places the full glass of beer in front of him, Jon mutters, "Not much going on today…"

She shakes her head. "Nope, it's slow this time of year. When hurricane season comes, tourists stay away."

"Is Ace around?"

"Ain't seen 'im yet today…" While Jon takes a big sip, Flora wipes the bar down. After tossing the towel over her shoulder she waves. "Holler if you need anything else, honey. I'll be in the back doing inventory."

He watches her stroll off, has another long sip of his beer, and then turns back to the uncrowded room. His gaze lingers on one of the empty booths along the far wall, and his thoughts drift to his recent dealings with Carlos, a local businessman from Cuba.

Jon sits quietly at the bar with his drink. When he sees a flash of daylight in the bar-back mirror and hears the door, he excitedly turns just in time to see the tourist couple leaving. Disappointed, he turns back and takes another sip of his drink. "The vacation-honeymoon is over I guess..."

He has one last swig, takes out a five-dollar bill and places it under the half-finished glass. Jon slides off the stool, makes his way to the door and leaves.

# IV

The streets are still puddled from the recent storm, and dark, gloomy skies threaten more rain. Strolling through Old Town, Jon notices that, with no cruise ships due to arrive, the strip along Duval Street is empty. He peers into a shop window and notices the salesclerk reading a book.

Cutting down a narrow side street, Jon walks toward the Clipped Kitty again. He stops outside the elaborate iron front gate and looks to the well-maintained gardens on the property. His wandering gaze travels to the second story stained-glass windows, and he wonders what exotic women inside might be spying down at him in the street. Knowing that there is ready companionship just inside, Jon feels a tingle of excitement.

From behind, a familiar voice suddenly startles him from his amorous musings. "Lookin' for passion, writer-man?"

# Dominica Dash

Jon turns to see the teenager, Casey Kettles, wearing his usual, yellow-framed sunglasses, grinning snarkily at him. "Hey, Casey… Just passing by…"

"Again?"

Jon realizes that the kid must have seen him stop earlier on his way to the Conch Tavern. "Figured I'd check to see if Rollie's truck was out front."

"It's not."

Jon gazes around. "Yeah, I see that."

Casey gives him a snide look and slips around him to open the front gate. "*Nobody's* around today…"

"I heard Rollie is on a trip."

"So what?" Casey points to the Conch Train logo on his staff shirt. "Without any tourists to fleece, they don't need anyone to drive the stupid train around."

Staring at Casey's uniform, Jon asks, "You have a job?"

"We can't *all* sit on our butts at the Conch or loaf around all day pretending to write. Besides, it's the best place to scope out the newbies in town."

Pondering the idea of Casey actually having a real job, Jon looks down the quiet, palm-lined street. "Have you seen Carlos around?"

"He's in Cuba right now, taking care of some really *important* business."

The youth makes air quotes with his fingers and, even though Jon can't see the kid's eyes behind the dark sunglasses, he can tell they roll with sarcasm. Jon glances down the street again and then looks to his wristwatch to make sure it hasn't been stolen. He nods to the snarky teenager. "Well, I guess I'll see you around sometime."

"Not if I see you first."

As Casey steps through the front gate, he calls after Jon. "Hey there, writer-man...! You should come in for a quick fling. Since times are slow, the girls might give you a good discount. Could put some ink in your pen...!"

Disregarding the uncouth comment, Jon walks away. Lifting a hand to wave, he glances back at the youth. "See ya..."

~*~

Jon checks the mailbox on the gate before entering the yard to the estate where he stays. Flipping through the pile of junk mail and flyers, he spots an envelope addressed to him. His curiosity aroused, Jon moves it to the top of the stack.

Entering the apartment, Jon tosses the junk mail into the trash bin beside the doorway. He carefully looks the letter over. The return address is from France with the name *J. Renee'* printed above it. He taps the envelope on his palm and mutters, "A letter from Jeanee' Renee'...?"

Looking through the open doorway to the landlord's house, he suddenly feels apprehensive. Slowly, he opens the letter and slides a handwritten note from the envelope. It reads:

*Hello Jonathan,*

*I know we haven't yet had the pleasure of meeting in person, but I need to ask a favor of you. In a few weeks, I will be receiving the delivery of a valuable piece of artwork. The problem is, because of customs paperwork and a series of unfortunate events, the piece will arrive to the island of Dominica. I need someone I can trust to accept the piece and supervise its journey home to my residence in Key West. I am providing an airline ticket and a local contact on the island. Thank you for your help with this matter.*

*Sincerely,*
*Jeanee' Renee'*

Jon takes two items out of the envelope. One is a card with a telephone number scribbled on it and the name, *Raul*. The other is an airline ticket issued in Jon's name. In disbelief, he stares at the flight's departure date. "In a *few weeks…? Damn… This* is for *tomorrow!*"

Jon reads the letter over again. Skeptical, and unsure of what she is asking him to do, he's not sure who to approach to verify the odd request. He moves to the phone by the couch, lifts the handset and fingers the rotary dial.

A gruff voice answers. "*Yello…* Key West Air Charters."

"Hello, Ace. It's Jon."

"Hey, Jon… What's up? You in trouble again?"

"Uh, I don't think so…"

The mechanic chuckles. "Heck, I'm jest pullin' yer leg. What can I do fer ya?"

"When is Rollie due back?"

"Uhhh, he jest left on a trip to the islands yesterday, so… I don't know. Maybe a week…?"

Jon glances down to scan the handwritten note from his mysterious landlord. "Do you know where Dominica is?"

"If it's not the Dominican Republic yer talkin' about, there's an island jest to the north of Martinique called Dominica, which is pronounced, *Daa-muh-neeca*."

"Do you know anything about the place?"

The mechanic is quiet for a moment. "It's jest an island like the rest of 'em in the Lower Antilles. Mostly bananas, beaches, and tourists... Why? Are you lookin' to go on holiday from yer life on vacation?" Ace laughs good-humoredly, but when Jon doesn't answer, he adds, "I'm jest kiddin' ya, kid. What's goin' on?"

"I might have to travel there. On business..."

"Really? What kinda business would *that* be?"

Jon looks around his tastefully furnished apartment and considers his rent-free arrangement. "Do you know the woman who owns the property where I stay?"

"Jeanee' Renee'? I met her once at some charity thing. Yeah... She's a bit of a kook, but nice enough."

"She needs me to do her a favor. She sent a letter asking me to pick something up in Dominica." The phone line goes silent, and Jon thinks the call might have disconnected. "Hello...? *Ace*...?"

"Yeah..."

"What do you think?"

"Sounds kinder strange..."

"Which part...?"

"Havin' to personally pick up somethin' in a third-world country fer someone you haven't ever met..."

The mechanic's perspective gives Jon second thoughts. He glances to his computer on the table, then back at the gloomy day outside. "Yes, it *is* a bit odd, but

I've been staying at her place for free. On the recommendation of a friend…"

"Well, everything has a price."

"What should I do?"

"Rollie probably won't be back until late next week. When d'ya need to be there fer the pickup?"

"She sent me an airline ticket for tomorrow."

"Tomorrow, huh? Not wastin' any time… Ya have a place to stay down there?"

Jon looks at the card. "She gave me the name and contact number of a local person." On the other end of the line, Ace goes quiet. Jon can hear him breathing, so he waits a moment. Finally, he asks, "What do you think?"

"This is more *Rollie's* sorta thing. Goin' off somewheres half-cocked and not havin' any details… But, what the hell… Might as well do it. What could go wrong?"

Jon nods his head half-heartedly, as he looks at his name on the airline ticket and then back to the letter, "Thanks Ace… I'll let you know how it goes over a beer at the Conch."

"Sure thing… Be careful…"

Jon hangs up and looks to the empty travel bag slumped in the corner. "Yeah… What could go wrong?"

# V

As the sun sets over the island of Key West, a cool tropical breeze hints of the coming rain. While walking down a street in a quaint neighborhood a few blocks from his apartment, Jon listens to the competing sounds of traffic and barroom music. Hearing the clanking of a rusty bike chain, Jon turns to see a Beach Cruiser bicycle coming directly at him. Hoping it might be his friend, Aston, Jon reacts with disappointment as a lone tourist pedals by.

Continuing his evening walk, Jon eventually crosses Duval Street. He looks down the main avenue to see only a few people moving from bar to bar or heading home after enjoying live music. Being the off-season, this is not what the usual tourist nightlife looks like. For a moment, he wonders which version of this island paradise he likes better.

Arriving at the Conch Republic Tavern, Jon stops outside the garden patio. He notices that, due to the storm, the chairs are all wet, and the tables have tree debris on them. Staring up at the carved, wooden sign above the door, Jon murmurs to himself. "Rollie and Angie are off on some trip, most of the tourists are gone, and even Carlos is out of town. Nothing but an empty barstool and loneliness waiting for me in there..." Deciding not to go in, he resumes his walk.

Taking a roundabout route back home, Jon ends up in front of the Clipped Kitty again. Catching the scent of Jasmine wafting through the air, he scans the gaudy, old place and its lush gardens accented by gothic-inspired landscape lighting. The hairs on his arms prickle and, smiling, he shakes his head. "My luck, I'd have that damn kid, Casey, running commentary from the next room." After a moment, he moves on.

~*~

Rays of morning light stream in through Jon's apartment window. His travel backpack sits on the coffee table, and next to it sits the letter, the airline ticket, and a small pile of clothes. Jon exits the bathroom with some flip-flops and a dop kit, and he tucks them into the bag. After stuffing the clothes in the bag, he looks to his laptop computer and considers taking it along. Speaking aloud to himself, he remarks, "Should only be gone a few days... If I lose my computer, I could lose months of work." His gaze travels around the room and then drifts outside to the tall palm trees swaying in the breeze. "And, all work and no play makes Jack a dull boy..."

Jon flips his backpack's cover flap over and fastens the straps. He picks up the letter and ticket from his landlord and, before tucking them both into his pocket, checks to make sure the contact number is still there. He looks around the room. "You don't get to choose adventure; adventure chooses you." With that thought in mind, he heads out the door, closes it behind him and starts his hike to the airport.

~*~

Inside Key West International Airport, Jon sits waiting. Checking the schedule board, he sees that his flight has been delayed one hour. Glancing down at his travel bag, he shakes his head. "I should have brought a book."

Jon gets up, slings his backpack over his shoulder and walks to a kiosk with Key West t-shirts, snacks and magazines. On a book turnstile, he spots some pocket paperbacks with flashy titles and adventure-styled covers. Quickly recognizing his pen name, *J. T. Springs*, he wanders over to see the display.

Book titles range from African adventures to treasure hunting in the South Pacific, with a few Westerns sprinkled in. Jon smiles to himself, selects one of the paperbacks and flips it over to read the back. There is no author photo, but the brief biography reads:

*Mystery/Adventure novelist, J. T. Springs has written dozens of bestsellers in almost every genre. He is known for his historical adventure stories that have been translated into several languages and published all around the world. He writes with a Remington portable typewriter, and his whereabouts are unknown.*

# Eric H. Heisner

Jon returns the book and looks to the top of the display, where an advertisement announces that his newest volume is to be released soon. Jon casually mutters, "I can't say that Moselly isn't doing his job well. He knows how to sell books."

An older, overly tan lady in a tube-top nudges past him and reaches out for one of the South American-themed titles showing a sweaty adventurer saving a half-dressed woman in an Incan ruin. She smiles at Jon and holds the paperback up. "You *can't* go wrong with any of these *Springs* books."

He smiles back at her. "You like to read his stuff?"

"I'll read 'em again and again, until the covers fall off. This one here is one of my absolute favorites. He's got another book coming out real soon."

"I thought people only read books on electronic devices these days."

The lady flashes a toothy, way-too-white grin at him. "Trust me, I've tried those things. It got beach sand in the cracks and didn't last long. These small paperbacks are the way to go. I fly up north to see my daughter and grand-babies twice a year, and I *always* grab one on the way. Believe it or not, there's a new J. T. Springs *Fan-club* in Michigan, because I leave my copies there for my daughter to share."

Jon smiles and flushes a little. "That's pretty cool."

The lady gives him a wink and heads to the register. "Try any one of them out. You can't go wrong with a little armchair adventure."

Grabbing a paperback that has a tropical, Caribbean-looking cover, titled *Guns over Grenada*, he vaguely remembers the gun-running pirate storyline from years back. He takes it to the cash register and sets it down along with some chocolate-covered peanuts.

As the tanned lady finishes with her purchases, she looks over to see which book Jon chose. She smiles and runs her tongue along the front of her teeth. "That's a *really juicy* one… Good stuff! It has some *fantastic* love scenes in it."

Jon blushes with embarrassment. "Oh, yeah…?"

"What's a great adventure without some good sex?" Smiling flirtatiously, she hikes up her sagging tube top and saunters away with her book and a tiny bottle of wine.

Jon exchanges an uncomfortable look with the cashier and grins innocently. "She seems to be a fan of reading."

As the cashier rings Jon up, he looks at the book's cover, over to the *J. T. Springs* display, and then back to the paperback. He gives Jon a nod and tears off the receipt. "Have a nice day… Don't get into *too* much adventure, though. These Key West grannies know how to have a good time."

Jon tucks the receipt inside his book, grabs the candy and turns toward his flight gate. "Thanks…"

CONCH REPUBLIC

1828

KEY WEST

30

# VI

Boarding for the flight to Dominica begins, and Jon lowers the paperback novel to his lap. He has already read a dozen pages, so he tucks the register receipt in to mark his place. Next to him, a man gets up to join the line of boarding passengers. He smiles at Jon and gestures to the book. "Good book…?"

"Uh, yeah… Pretty good, so far…"

"I've read a few of his adventure stories." Unsure if he's a fan or not, Jon nods and listens, as the man continues. "They're like going to one of those upscale restaurant chains. The meal is decent, you know exactly what you're gonna get, and they're satisfying enough to have you wanting to come back again someday."

Turning the paperback over to look at the cover image, Jon thinks a second, and then looks back at the man. He asks, "You ever wish the stories were different? Or, more serious…?"

"Why? People read those sort of books to be entertained, and his stuff does that perfectly." He looks to the line of people moving out to the airplane. "You headed to Dominica?"

"Yeah."

"This is us…"

Holding his book at his side, Jon slings his backpack over his shoulder and follows the man toward the check-in line. When boarding the plane, he moves past the man he talked to earlier and nods to him. Jon finds his seat and looks out the window at the Key West Airport. Before the stewardess finishes her seatbelt and safety message, he takes a baseball cap out of his bag and places it over his face. Jon closes his eyes, takes a deep breath and drifts off. By the time the airplane is in flight, Jon is already in writer-dreamland.

~*~

Turbulence causes the commercial airliner to shake. With a start, Jon wakes and takes the hat from over his eyes. Looking out the window, he sees clear skies and blue waters. Jon checks his wristwatch, calculating how long he has been asleep and how much flight time is left.

The airplane shakes again, and the *fasten your seatbelts* light pops on. Several people in the aisle move to take their seats, and the stewardess rushes past collecting any garbage. The plane trembles violently, and the attendant is nearly knocked off her feet. She braces herself against the seat-backs, as the plane dips and tilts. Over the intercom, the captain's voice announces, "*Please take your seats. On approach to Dominica, we will be battling a strong crosswind coming over the ocean.*"

# Dominica Dash

As the stewardess rushes to her jump-seat in the back, the airplane tilts sharply and quickly rights itself again. Passengers, holding on to their armrests, squeal and gasp, while the view through their windows shifts suddenly between land and blue sky. As Jon peers out his own window at a lush, green island below, a window shade, a few seats up, slams shut.

The commercial airliner cruises right past the small group of islands and continues to reduce altitude as it approaches the next landmass. With a long approach, it looks like the aircraft will smash directly into the tropical island ahead of it. Zooming over the rocky coastline, the airplane veers between two mountain peaks and cruises over the jungle.

As the air turbulence continues, the airplane's wingtips teeter from side to side, prompting more anxious cries from the passengers. A strong gust pushes the airplane nearly sideways, and everyone is pulled down into their seats, as the pilot expertly corrects for the blasting wind currents. Jon murmurs, "I think I'm more comfortable flying low and slow with Rollie."

A heavy, dark-skinned woman seated next to him looks over and chuckles. "Dis is da usual air bumps into Dominica. Not many crashes…" Jon forces a smile and turns to look out the window, as the jungle canopy continues to creep closer. Ahead, a small airport finally comes into view, and the airliner quickly descends to the runway. As the wheels bounce, skid, and then settle on the pavement, the relieved passengers clap and cheer.

Jon looks to the island woman next to him and exclaims, "Wow…! You say it's always like that?!"

"Sometimes much worse… Dey buildin' a bigg'r airport, but it only means more airplanes git to take da bumpy ride."

Turning to the window again, Jon watches as the plane taxis toward the gate. A set of passenger stairs is pulled over, and a what looks to be a riding lawnmower tows a luggage cart. He tucks his hat into his backpack and takes out the letter with the contact number for Raul. "I wonder if they still have pay-phones here…"

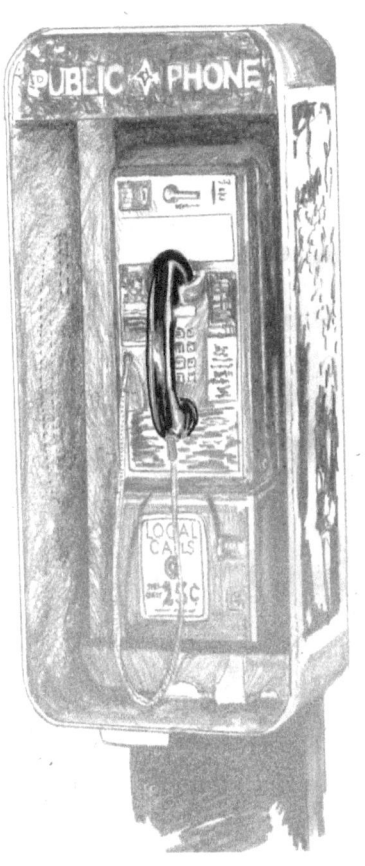

# VII

Walking through the small international airport, Jon keeps an eye out for a public payphone. He spots one just beyond the baggage claim and heads toward it. Before reaching the phone, as he feels his pockets for coins, he is intercepted by a tall stranger holding a placard with the name *Jonathan Springer* printed across it.

Jon stops and looks at the islander. "I'm Jon Springer. Are you Raul?"

"Yes, I am. I'm sure glad ta find ya made da flight okay. Da boss-lady say maybe ya come or maybe ya not."

"I'm here. Not sure exactly what I'm to do."

"I take care of *everyt'ing*."

Raul reaches out for Jon's backpack, but Jon declines. "That's okay… I'll carry it. I don't have any other bags."

# Dominica Dash

The guide smiles. "Boss-lady say ya'n adventia-man, and I see dat ya pack accordin'ly."

"Actually, I'm a writer."

"Ya write da real stuff, or make it up?"

"Fiction in the real world…"

Leading the way through the crowded airport terminal, Raul turns. "Ya be a writer like da Ernest Hemin'way?"

Following along, observing his surroundings, Jon nods. "Yeah… I'm working at it." Raul leads them outside to a six-person transport van. He opens the rear, passenger-side door and ushers Jon inside. Jon pauses and gestures to the front seat. "Could I sit up front?" Then he notices the steering wheel on the right-hand side. He exchanges a look with Raul, and the driver widens his eyes.

"Ya want ta drive?"

"No… I'm used to the wheel on the *other* side."

Unsure, the driver shrugs and tilts his head. "Fine by me, but da hotel won't like it. Dey want us ta treat ya very special."

"What hotel are we going to?"

Raul flashes a smile and puts up a finger to his lips. "Shhhh… It's a *secret* on da bay."

Jon climbs in back, and the driver pushes the door shut. As Raul moves forward to get in, Jon looks to the empty front seats and mutters to himself. "Great… I *love* a little mystery on my adventures."

~*~

Driving the coastal road, the van makes its way east, then south, to a secret getaway on the far side of the island. Through the windows, Jon sees jungle on one side and a rocky shoreline on the other. He leans forward to speak to Raul. "How far is it?"

"Not dat far…"

"Is this a large island?"

"Nope, not *dat* big… We almost dere…"

There is a security checkpoint at the entry to the resort, and the driver gives the guard a wave before the gate opens for them to pass through. They drive down a winding stretch of driveway that is immaculately landscaped to look like a cleaned-up version of natural jungle. Through the thick foliage, Jon can barely make out private bungalows that blend well with their surroundings.

They stop at the reception building and are greeted by a woman with a wooden platter holding an island drink and a cool washrag. Stepping out of the van, Jon reaches for the wet towel first. "Thank you."

"Mista Jonat'an Springa?"

"Yes."

"Welcome ta da secret getaway of our island."

Jon exchanges the cool towel for the drink and then reaches back into the van to grab his bag. "Thanks. It's nice to be here. What's the name of this place?"

The greeter puts a finger to her lips and smiles. "Shhhh… It's a *secret*."

"I bet it's printed on the bill."

She sets the platter aside and waves for him to follow. "No bill for Mista Springa… Everyt'ing is *all* taken care of. Come along. I will show ya to ya beach-view bungalow."

# Dominica Dash

Jon turns to Raul standing at the front of the van. "What's expected? Don't I have to pick something up?"

The driver waves him on and grins. "Go wit her and have a nice time. Worry not… I will take care of *everyt'ing.*"

Jon looks at his watch. "When will you let me know?"

"Few days, maybe…"

"*Days…?*"

Raul shrugs, as he steps around the van and opens the driver's door. "Who knows?"

"I was hoping *you* did."

The local merely laughs good-naturedly and gets back into the British-make van. He rolls down the window and calls, "See ya soon, Mista Springa."

As the van starts and then pulls away, Jon is left holding his bag and the welcome drink. He turns to the greeter, who is patiently waiting. "Follow you…?"

"D'ya need help wit ya luggage?"

He tastes the cocktail and slings his bag over his shoulder. "Nope… I got it."

Her smile lingers, as he takes another sip from the drink. "Would ya like anodda beverage?"

He looks at the tall glass that barely has a swallow taken from it and shakes his head. "No, I think I'm okay for now."

"Wondaful… Please come along wit me…"

He follows her down the combed-gravel walkway, through the tidy jungle landscaping, toward the beach and his private island bungalow.

# VIII

Jon is led into the quaint, but luxurious accommodations. First, they enter a screened-in area with a kitchen that looks out over the aqua-blue waters of the bay. He peeks into the adjoining room at a king size bed next to an open-air shower and bathtub. Noticing two robes on wall-hooks, he jokes, "It's very nice… Am I expecting anyone else?"

The greeter smiles apologetically and shakes her head. "We only have ya down as a single guest. Unless ya would *like* us ta include someone…"

"No, I was just making a joke."

She puts on a kind smile and, without further comment, gestures toward the kitchen counter. "Here is ya daily menu. Merely mark down what ya would like for each meal, and we will bring it t'ya. Or, if ya choose, ya can dine at da beach bar, or at our gourmet restaurant."

# Dominica Dash

Jon nods. Still benignly smiling, she continues. "Would ya like me ta show ya 'round da room?"

He looks around at the extravagant accommodations, which are even smaller than his garage apartment in Key West. "Looks simple enough…"

"I can show ya how ta use da coffee maker."

He shrugs. "I think I can figure it out."

Keeping up her constant smile, she moves to the door. "If dere is anyt'ing at all ya are in need of, please reach out." She gestures to a house phone, gives a bow and steps out.

Jon drops his bag onto a chair, glances at his drink and then out to the magnificent ocean view. "I guess I'm officially on vacation from my life on vacation."

~*~

The evening sun shines across the secluded bay, as Jon wanders down the gravel path toward the resort's beach bar. With no other guests around, he sits at a stool that faces out to the sunset. Shortly, the bartender comes over to him. "What can I get for ya?"

"What's the local beer?"

"Dominica's pride: *Kubuli*."

"Sure… I'll have one of those."

Reaching into a cooler, the bartender pulls out a green bottle with a green and red label. He pops the cap off and sets it in front of Jon. "Dere ya go…"

"Thanks."

Jon scoops up the bottle, lifts it to his lips, takes a swig, and then smiles approvingly at the ice-cold beverage. Attentive, the bartender asks, "How d'ya like it?"

"It's good and cold."

The bartender smiles back. "Dey make it in Roseau."

"Is that a nearby city?"

"It's our capitol, down da coast."

Jon has another big swallow and looks around the bar. He glances at his wristwatch and then turns to the bartender. "Kinda quiet around here."

"We do not have many guests dis time of year."

"The weather is really nice, and it's a beautiful place. Why not…?"

"It is always like dis during da hurricane season."

"*Hurricane* season…? When is *that*?"

The bartender puts on a show of being busy, as he cleans a bar glass. "During da summer, dey can happen anytime, but August ta early September most likely for dem."

Jon thinks about the time of year and looks to the sunset. "So, pretty much, right about *now*?"

"Not today…"

"When was the last bad one?"

He doesn't have to think very long before replying, "Maria was a category five 'n happened dis time of year."

"When was that?"

"Jest a few years ago… Two t'ousand seventeen, it was. Everyone who was here on da island knows where dey were when *dat* one happened."

"Scary…?"

"Ne'er so scared in my life, 'n I use-ta be *married*."

Jon grins. "Not married anymore?"

# Dominica Dash

"Dey say, *Happy Wife, Happy Life*, but for da husband, it's usually, *Happy Husband… We'll see 'bout dat.*"

Jon laughs and gazes out to the setting sun. "I know a guy with a place in the Yucatan, who would enjoy swapping marriage philosophies with you."

The bartender wipes the bar with a towel and smiles. "Comes wit da experience."

Looking around the empty beach bar again, Jon asks, "So, what's there to do around this place?"

"Dere's da secret beach…" The bartender continues, as Jon nods. "How long ya here for?"

"Maybe a few days…"

"Why da *maybe?* Headed somewhere else?"

"No, my plans are a little open-ended right now."

Tucking the towel away, the bartender puts both hands to the bar top, leans forward and looks down toward the cove. "Have paddleboards 'n kayaks. On da odder side of da island, dere are waterfalls and canyons t'explore. If ya ride horses, dey can take ya on a trip t'rough da jungle or on da beach."

Jon nods. "Riding horses on the beach sounds fun."

The bartender shrugs. "Sounds much more fun dan it is. Dey unsaddle ta lead your horse t'rough da small waves, and all ya end up wit is wet pants 'n a lame pony ride."

Disappointed, Jon has another sip from his drink and looks to the boathouse lined with kayaks. "Maybe I'll take a boat out tomorrow. To explore…"

"If ya like tours, ya can explore upriver wit Ice."

"Ice?"

"He's a local character. Very colorful... Grew up here. He knows everyone, and everyone knows him."

"What's upriver?"

"Lotsa trees, birds, insects... Oh, and dey shot one of dem pirate movies dere."

"Oh, yeah...? Which one?"

"I dunno... Da one wit da guy who had da crazy-scary wife dat sued him. I bet *he's* got some stories."

"Yeah, they are definitely not the role models for a long and happy marriage."

As the sun dips below the horizon, Jon leans back on the bar and takes in the fantastic view. He finishes his beer and slides the empty to the bartender. Before Jon can order another, the bartender reaches into the cooler and pulls one out.

"No, that's okay... I'm headed back."

The bartender pries open the top and slides it to Jon. "Take it wit you... I'll put it on da tab."

"Who's paying the tab?"

"It's *all* taken care of. Ya be our *all-star guest!*"

Jon sips from the cold bottle of Kubuli. "Looks like I'm your *only* guest." In the fading light, he gives a wave, slides from the stool and walks off toward the beach. As a warm, tropical breeze washes over him, he stops to take in the day's last hint of sunlight.

# IX

When he comes out to the screened porch, Jon is greeted by a breakfast display laid out on a table. Taking a croissant from the plate, he tests the freshness with a sniff and has a bite. Checking the ocean view, he notices that there is a wall of heavy clouds forming on the horizon.

Jon gets a whiff of chocolate from the steaming teapot. Curious, he pours himself a cupful and finds it to be a bitter, local dark cocoa. He grabs his book, takes a seat, and starts to read as he eats. After a while, he looks up, laughs to himself and puts the book aside. "Sitting here, reading my own book, is a strange experience. Kinda like talking to myself…"

As jungle parrots chatter outside, Jon refills his hot cocoa and looks to the room's telephone. Picking up the handset, he dials nine for the reception desk. After ringing several times, it finally picks up and a voice answers. "Hello, Mista Springa. What can I do for ya?"

"I was wondering if I had any calls or messages?"

"Are ya expectin' any?"

"Possibly…"

There is a brief pause, the sound of feet patting across the floor and the shuffle of papers. "Sorry, nottin' yet…"

Wondering what he's going to do to keep busy for the day, Jon glances outside. "Okay… Uh, I heard there are boat tours upriver somewhere nearby?"

"Oh, yes… Dat would be wit Ice."

"Is he doing any today?"

"I could set ya up for dis afternoon."

"Sure… Sounds like fun."

"Anyt'ing else?"

His gaze drifts to his paperback sitting on the table. "No… Just let me know if I get any calls."

"Yes, Mista Springa."

Jon hangs up, gazes out the screened windows and then sits back down with his book. He takes a deep breath and murmurs, "Not much else to do here but enjoy the solitude." Finishing off a muffin, Jon chews, has a drink from his mug and continues reading.

~*~

Still seated in the same chair, mouth agape and head tilted back, Jon is sleeping. The open paperback lies in his lap, and the breakfast dishes have been cleared from the table. Suddenly, when the phone rings, Jon jolts awake and blurts, "*Moselly*, what is it?!" Getting his bearings, he looks around the bungalow as the phone rings again. He reaches over and lifts the receiver. "Hello…?"

"Mista Springa?"

"Yes."

"Ya boat captain will be ready for ya in one hour."

Jon looks at his wristwatch, waits for his eyes to focus and nods. "One hour... Okay, that's fine."

"Have a nice time."

The telephone line clicks, and Jon hangs up the receiver. Rubbing his temples, he takes a moment to wake up entirely. Then, he marks his page and puts the book aside. "Guess I have time for a pre-river-cruise drink..."

On the walk to the beach bar, Jon notices that it is as empty as it was the evening prior. A different bartender smiles when she sees him approaching. Jon goes to the bar, takes a seat on the same stool he used yesterday and looks out at the ocean. Then, he places his elbows on the bar, smiles at the bartender, and orders. "I'll have a Kubuli."

The bartender opens a beer, sets it on the bar and puts on her welcoming smile again. "Are ya havin' a nice time?"

Jon shrugs. "I guess so. Kinda quiet around here."

"Yes, most people come to dis secret spot ta get away from da rest of da world."

"Yeah, I can see that... Most of the time, when I travel, it's to see *more* of the world."

The bartender tidies up a few items behind the counter. "We can get ya a driver ta show ya 'round da island."

Jon takes a drink from his beer and looks over to the beach shack. "I'm headed out on a riverboat trip with Ice."

# Dominica Dash

At the mention of the boatman's name, the bartender gets a peculiar look in her eye. Jon notices it for only a moment, before it's gone, and she remarks, "It will be a very nice time. Do ya have ya site pass already?"

"No... What's that?"

"It's our government's met'od of charging tourists for da enjoyment of da natural resources."

"The front desk set the trip up."

"Dey will prob'ly have one ready for ya. Just be sure ta bring it along, or dey will not let ya proceed."

"I hear tourism is really slow this time of year because of the chance of hurricanes."

"Yes, but dat does not keep da wealt'y Chinese and Middle-Easterners from comin'."

Jon notices the bartender's change of tone and counters, "This is a long way for the Chinese to come for a vacation."

Nervously checking over her shoulder to see if anyone else is listening, the bartender apologetically shakes her head. "Sorry... I should not be talkin' about such t'ings."

"Why?"

"Certain people would not approve."

"Who's to say?"

"Where dere is much profit ta be made, dere are many eyes and ears who would want ta report me."

Jon is about to ask more, but the phone suddenly rings. The bartender picks it up and listens without saying anything. Eventually, she puts down the receiver and looks over to Jon. "I must go. Would ya like anodda drink before I leave?"

He looks down at his fresh beer and shakes his head. "Uh...No, I'm fine, thanks." Jon has a sip from the bottle, as he watches her pack a few items and depart. Glancing at the time, he scans the seemingly vacant resort. "Just when I thought this place couldn't be any more empty..."

Jon hears the hum of a boat motor approaching and looks out to the bay. Coming around the point, a single-engine vessel bounces through the waves, heading toward the beach. Near the boathouse dock, he sees a man in a hotel staff shirt step out to wave him over. Jon looks around, unsure of who is being waved at, until he hears the man call out. *"Mista Springa,* ya river boat is comin'..."

Jon takes another swig of beer, slips off the stool and makes his way toward the boathouse.

# X

$A$s Jon walks up to the dock staffer, he smiles and takes another sip of his beer. He points the neck of the bottle out to the approaching motorboat and asks, "Is that *Ice* coming?"

With a grin, the staff member offers a slip of paper and a small cooler with a rolled towel on top. "Dat is Ice. Here is ya site pass and a cooler with da snacks and refreshment."

Jon finishes his beer and trades the glass bottle for the pass, towel and cooler. He then looks down the empty beach and out to the approaching boat. "Am I the only one going?"

"Yes, Mista Springa… Ya have a special private tour." Jon follows the man out into the water and waits, as Ice cuts the engine and uses a paddle to get closer to shore.

Knee deep in the rolling surf, Jon turns and looks back to the resort. "Are there any *other* guests staying here?"

The staff member nods and beams a joyful smile at Jon. "Yes, *many* people stay here."

"Where *are* they?"

He puts a finger to his lips, shushing. "It's a *secret*."

Jon considers the peculiar answer, as he wades over to the boat and climbs in. Looking like a skinny sea pirate from the movies, Ice greets him warmly. "Hallo, dere! Welcome to da river cruise. I'm *Ice,* yer cap'n."

Situating himself on one of the boat's wooden benches, Jon looks to the beach where the dock staffer waves gleefully. Turning to the boat captain, Jon replies, "Hello, Ice. I'm Jon."

"Nice ta meet ya, Mista Jon." Ice paddles the boat out past the rolling breakers and then lowers the outboard motor into the water. "Be dere shortly... Sit back 'n enjoy da ride..." The engine sputters to life, pushing the slender watercraft across the swelling waves and out past the sliver of land that protects the hidden bay.

~*~

Water splashes over the bow, as Ice steers the boat through choppy waves along the coastline. He taps Jon on the shoulder, then points ahead to a wide inlet where a river flows out to the sea. The smokey smell of campfire cooking comes from the rocky shoreline, where two children cast fishing lines. "Dats where we goin'... T'ree-hundred-sixty-five rivers flow on da island of Dominica. One ta explore every day of da year."

Jon inhales the pleasant odor of the cook-fire and studies the boys on the shore. "We should have brought fishing gear."

Ice shakes his head. "No, sir... No one is allowed ta fish on dese rivers. Dem kids catch da ones dat come out of da river, but no one can go furder up."

"Why no fishing?"

"Da Government made it a law."

Jon sits back thoughtfully, thinking that he understands. "Oh, protecting the environment..."

"I'd like ta t'ink so, but mostly ta control da people."

The boat arrives at the mouth of the river and pulls up alongside another old wooden vessel. Ice gives a shrill whistle, and a man comes out of a waterside shack, chewing a mouthful and wiping his hands on his stained t-shirt. Ice calls out to him. "Joe, we go up da river taday. How's t'ings?" Turning to Jon, Ice holds out his hand. "D'ya have da site pass?"

Jon pulls the slip of paper out of his pocket and hands it to Ice, who shows it to the man. The attendant, still chewing, nods before swallowing. "T'ings good. Nice day for a boat ride. Nobody else up dere."

Ice smiles, tilts his chin to the local in a goodbye gesture, and then hands the pass back to Jon. "Okay, mon. See ya lata'."

The river attendant waves and heads back to his shack at the end of the pier. After pushing off from the other boat, Ice guns the outboard motor and steers them upriver.

~*~

# Eric H. Heisner

Flying over clear, blue waters, a WWII vintage Grumman seaplane comes around on approach to one of the many islands in the Lesser Antilles. Seated at the controls, Rollie reaches up to adjust the overhead engine throttles, as he prepares to make a water landing.

Angie, wearing a pair of cut-off jean shorts and a tight-fitting Key West Air Charters shirt, sits in the copilot seat. She looks over at Rollie, as she speaks into her headset microphone. "Let's try to get back before the end of the week, so I can throw that party for Jon's book release." Momentarily distracted, Rollie glances at her. "Yeah…? His book's come out already?"

"This week, I think…"

Rollie returns his focus to the task of landing on water. Through his headphones, he mutters, "Have you read it?"

"Not yet…"

"Wonder if it's any good…"

She watches below for any obstacles in their path. "Doesn't matter… It's an accomplishment just to write one."

Rollie shrugs. "Heck, some big-time authors put out several books in a year."

Nearing an island village spread out along the shoreline, Angie smirks and stares ahead as they decrease in altitude, "Everyone can't be a prolific author like Clive Cussler, or… Who's that other guy you like to read? *J. T. Springs*…?"

"I think Cussler died."

"Hasn't stopped new books from coming out…"

# Dominica Dash

Rollie glances at her and grins. "No, it hasn't…" Laughing, he adds, "That's not *all* I read."

She rolls her eyes. "Yeah, that *Water Flying* magazine…"

"I just look at the pictures."

"Figured as much…"

Keeping both hands firmly on the yoke, Rollie scans their ocean runway, while descending to the water's surface. "Heck, if we don't have any unexpected stops, we should be back in Key West by midweek."

"Thanks… I appreciate it."

The hull of the flying boat touches down on the water, skims over the aqua-blue waves and then settles in on the step. Zooming across the Caribbean waters, the amphibious plane steers toward the beachfront village.

# XI

On the river, surrounded by jungle, Ice steers the boat near to a tree limb hanging over the water and picks a single leaf. Crumpling it, he gives it a sniff and hands it forward to Jon. "Smells nice, eh? Ya can make good tea wit dat one."

Inhaling the pleasant aroma, Jon nods and feels the urge for a drink. He opens the provided cooler and peeks inside. "What do you think they sent along for me here?" Reaching in, he takes out a chilled bottle of Kubuli beer. Seeing another one, he offers it to Ice. "Would you like a beverage?"

"No, t'anks... I'm workin'."

Jon cracks off the cap on the bottle, puts it to his lips and has a swallow. "I'm sort of on vacation."

"What ya escapin' from?"

"Just life, I guess."

"Dis is a real good place ta do it. Dere's plenty of nutting to do 'round here."

"Things will get busier with the new airport, I suppose."

Ice spits over the side of the boat and several fish surface to check it out. "Dat for da gover'ment ta make more money, not for da good of da people."

"Why's that?"

Taking pause, the captain looks around for a moment. "It is not fer me ta say."

"Why not?"

"My personal opinions are not popular wit da ones who run our country. I grew up here and have seen many changes."

Interested, Jon leans closer. "Like what...?"

"Da Chinese... and da Middle-Easterners, wit lots of money who come here ta be citizens."

Confused, Jon takes a swig from his bottle and asks, "Why would Chinese people come here to be citizens?"

Ice shakes his head and lowers his voice, as his eyes scan the jungle along the shore. "I say too much already, 'n will get myself in trouble."

Jon opens the cooler, reaches in and pulls out the other bottle of beer. Jokingly, he offers it. "How about you have a cold one and tell me more about it?"

"No, t'anks, but I *will* tell you dat dis island is bein' sold out from under us."

"How so? I heard from my airport driver that the new hospital was donated back to the people."

Disgusted, the boatman rolls his eyes, and he glances over his shoulder as if someone might be listening. "We have a *Citizenship by Investment* program set up 'ere in Dominica… But, it only serves as a working front for wealt'y businessmen 'n terrorists ta get our national passports, 'n a way ta have backdoor access ta odda countries."

"Really… How?"

"We are a commonwealt'. Once upon a time, we travel freely to da United Kingdom for da education of our children. Now, anyone wit money buy demselves a Dominica passport, and dere are travel restrictions placed on *all* of *us* now for *security* purposes."

"You can just *purchase* citizenship here?"

"Almost…"

"How?"

Feeling paranoid, Ice takes a breath and peers around. "Investments like da hospital 'n da airport allows many people who are not from here ta use our country as an entry point for dere expanding businesses."

"Terrorists, too…?"

"Yes… Dey use *our* passport ta get ta many places where dere *own* would get questioned."

Jon listens with fascination. Gazing out to the dense jungle, he wonders if, as Ice seems to portray, anyone could actually be out there, in the undergrowth, spying on them. "How did this come to pass?"

Ice waves his arms out toward the shore of the river. "Once upon a time, dis whole coast was covered in bananas dat we harvested and sold. Den, dey saw bigger money in tourism, so we tried dat. But, us bein' in da hurricane belt is not a t'ing to put on da vacation brochure."

"I heard it's hurricane season now…"

"Yes, da rains and wind can sweep over us at any time. Dat is why ya are on yer own personal tour. Dere is not many tourists dat come to us dis time of year."

"Without tourists, the government attracts terrorists?"

"Dey are selling our little country out, piece by piece, and telling da people it is good for everyone." The boat chugs along at a slow pace, as Ice steers them toward the middle of the river. "When a terrible storm takes away yer house, da government give ya a new one."

"That's good…"

"No… Ya do not *own* da new one. You are now a servant to da state. Dey say you be grateful and vote da way dey tell ya, but now dey have taken away home ownership, and da property dat ya could've passed along ta yer children is now owned by da controlling politicians. Slowly, dey are makin' us all slaves to da masta, like in da olden days."

Processing what the boatman is telling him, Jon starts to understand the level of corruption that the people here have to deal with. Finished with his drink, he puts the empty bottle in the cooler. He looks at Ice and asks, "What can be done?"

The captain shrugs and looks up at the clouds in the sky. "T'ings will work out, eventually. Dey will get much worse, before people wake up 'n get upset 'nough ta want ta do somet'ing 'bout it. But, when it bad, sometimes it's too late."

# Eric H. Heisner

"Is anyone doing something about it?"

"I support da ones dat organize reform against what is being put upon us. And, I do my own t'ing... A little at a time." He gives a sly wink, and Jon isn't sure what to make of it.

"I'm just here for a few days to help out a friend."

"Ya n'er know..."

Puzzled, Jon replies, "What do you mean by that?"

Ice points out the dark clouds forming on the western horizon. "Da bad storms usually blow in from dat direction. N'er know when dey might form up 'n give us a good visit." Jon pivots to look at the sky, as Ice adds, "When dey blow in, ya n'er know what it will come wit."

Feeling a chilling breeze sweep over him, Jon sighs. "With *my* luck, I'll *surely* end up with a visit..."

# XII

Back at the resort's secluded beach, Jon steps off the boat and into the surf. Ice extends his hand over the port gunwale. "Mista Spring, it was a pleasure spendin' da day wit ya."

Jon shakes the calloused hand of the boat captain and, with a grin, replies, "Thanks for the informative river tour." There isn't anyone at the boathouse to welcome him, so he figures that the dock shack is probably closed for the evening. He wades through the knee-deep water to the shore and checks his wristwatch, noticing that it is after five in the afternoon. Behind him, the loud buzz of the outboard motor fades away, as Ice steers his boat out of the cove.

Carrying the resort cooler and towel, Jon makes his way up the beach and then sits in a lounge chair. He takes out his last beer and a paper bag of plantain chips. "No need to let this get warm..." Alone, watching the sunset, Jon enjoys his beverage and island snack.

~*~

The sun has dipped below the horizon, and the arrival of night has thousands of insects chattering in the jungle trees. Jon walks up the beach to the bar and notices that no one is around there either. There is a single lamp illuminating the bar, but it looks closed. Straining to see clearly in the dim light, he mutters, "I'm starting to think I really *am* the only guest here."

Jon decides to head to his bungalow. Continuing down the path, he is relieved to find ground lights leading the way. Jon climbs the stairs to the entryway, steps inside, and searches for a light switch.

Suddenly, a lamp on the other side of the room clicks on, and Jon is greeted by two officers in military S.W.A.T. attire. Jon breaks into a nervous sweat, unsure of what trouble he has stumbled into this time. "Uh, hello...? Is something going on?"

From the bedroom, a male voice answers and a suited gentleman steps out. "That is what *we* would like to know."

"Uh... Who are you?"

Flashing an official-looking badge, the man explains, "I'm with the Ministry of Security, Defense & Trade for the Island of Dominica."

Jon takes a moment to process the title and then asks, "Okay... Why are you here?"

# Dominica Dash

"*We* will be asking the questions..." The man flips a passport open and reads, "Jonathan T. Springer." He looks directly at Jon. "What does the *T* stand for?"

Scanning the room, Jon considers the armed soldiers. Then, he notices his few possessions spread out across the bed after having been searched. He mutters, "T is for *Trouble*..." When the government agent gives him a cold stare without even a hint of amusement, Jon asks, "What's going on...?"

"Please gather your belongings and come with us."

Glancing outside, then back at the screened doorway, Jon considers running, but then realizes he's got nowhere to go. "Why do I need to bring my stuff?"

"If we find you the least bit uncooperative, it could take a very long while to sort things out."

"Do I have a choice in this matter?"

The agent tucks Jon's passport into his suit pocket and pats it with his hand. "No, Mister Springer, you do not.

~*~

Jon is seated in the back of a black SUV, with the agent sitting beside him and the two soldiers up front. Jon peers through the dark-tinted windows to the flood lights at the resort gate as they pass through it. "Why am I being detained?"

The agent turns to Jon, sighs, and keeps his voice low. "Silence is best. Save your questions for the Chief Inspector."

"Why? What did I do?"

"Sir, it is not what you might, or might not have *done*… It is what you plan to *do*."

"I haven't done *anything*. Or, even *plan* to…"

"Most give that response…"

Getting nowhere, Jon decides to keep quiet and looks out the side window at the dark countryside. His thoughts drift to his most recent adventures, and then to the fact that he doesn't have any friends near that could come to his rescue. Feeling terribly alone, Jon takes a deep breath, slumps down in the seat and awaits his fate.

# XIII

At the Ministry of Security, Defense & Trade, Jon is escorted into a windowless, brick building and ushered to a room at the end of a long hallway. A soldier puts the bag of Jon's few belongings on the table in the middle of the room, then retreats to the corner next to the closed door. Jon looks around the interrogation room and has a seat on one of the metal chairs.

An hour passes silently, as Jon sits waiting in the room. He watches the guard standing casually by the entrance. Finally, footsteps approach, and the door opens to reveal a grey-haired man. The Chief Inspector steps in and looks at Jon. "Hello, Mister Springer..."

Jon sits up and waits for him to move closer, then asks, "Why am I here?"

# Dominica Dash

"A lot of questions have arisen since your arrival... Mostly concerning you."

Jon is confused. "I haven't got any answers."

"Why are you on the island of Dominica?"

"I'm on vacation."

"From what...?"

"What do you mean?"

"What is your occupation?"

From the inspector's callous tone, Jon gets the idea that this meeting is not off to a good start. "Uh, I'm a writer."

The Chief Inspector paces slowly around the room. "What sort of commentaries do you write?"

"I write books. About travel and adventure, mostly..."

The inspector goes to Jon's backpack on the table, opens the flap, and unpacks the contents. "So... You are a journalist. What are the locations of these books you write?"

"Actually, I mostly write fiction."

With a nod, he takes the J. T. Springs novel from the bag. Looking at the cover, he then turns it over to read the backside. "They say that most fiction stories have a hint of truth."

"Who says that?"

The inspector stops and studies Jon with piercing eyes. "Far too often, truth follows fiction."

Jon glances at the paperback in the inspector's hand. "Am I being suspected of gun-running?"

"Are you smuggling firearms?"

"No."

# Eric H. Heisner

After thumbing through the pages, the inspector places the book aside and continues to pull items from Jon's bag. "How about paintings...?"

A cold chill runs up Jon's spine, as he shakes his head. "Uh, I don't have any *artwork* in there."

Feigning a smile, the inspector stands up straight, adjusts his tie, and stares at Jon. "We are but a small country. Because of our limited economics, other countries think they can use us for their nefarious deeds."

"Do you mean using your Citizenship by Investment program to import illegal merchandise and people?"

"There are many forms of working around the system."

"I'm not a part of *any* of that."

The smile fades, but the cold, piercing eyes remain fixed. "Mister Springer, why are you here?"

"Like I said... I'm on vacation."

Having emptied the bag, the inspector considers the meager belongings on the table. "For a tourist, you pack light."

"I'm only staying a few days."

The inspector looks at Jon for a moment and then asks, "Who was it that bought your airline ticket?"

"A friend..."

"The well-funded entity that put you up at the resort?" Jon slowly nods, and the inspector resumes his questioning. "Who *is* this person that is so generous to you?" Not wishing to implicate himself, Jon keeps quiet. The inspector suggests, "You see... We would like to know *more* about this mysterious friend of yours."

# Dominica Dash

Jon looks at both the mirrored wall and the guard by the door before muttering, "I think I need a lawyer."

"What for...? You said you have done nothing wrong."

"You can ask *them* your questions."

The inspector scratches his neck, paces around the table and, while passing behind Jon, glances at the guard by the door. "Mister Springer, we want to know *who* you *work* for... And, more importantly, *why* your presence on our island brings up so many troubling questions."

Jon shrugs feebly. "I don't know what to tell you."

The officer moves to the door, opens it, gestures the guard to step outside with him, and then looks back at Jon. "Unfortunately, Mister Jon Springer, you will be here a while. That is, at least until you decide to cooperate fully with us..." About to close the door and leave, he pops his head back in to comment on one more thing. "Back in the good old days, we had ways to speed up this process. Primitive tactics were used, and information was relayed much more freely."

"You mean *torture...*?"

The inspector grins. "Merely forms of persuasion..."

Jon stares at him, until the door swings shut and is locked from the outside. He looks at his belongings spread out over the table, leans on his elbows, and then lays his head on a pile of his clothes.

# XIV

The airport shuttle van sits in front of the reception area of the beach club resort. The grey skies over the secluded bay are darkening with heavy storm clouds and spitting mists of rain. Raul comes out of the front office looking very disturbed. Glancing around suspiciously, he circles the van once, gets in and drives off.

~*~

There are no windows in the interrogation room to indicate whether it is night or day. Feeling his stomach growl, Jon looks at his watch. His clothes are folded on the table and stacked beside his personal items. Inspecting his belongings, Jon murmurs, "Wonder when they serve breakfast?"

There is a knock on the door, and Jon waits for it to open. Raul steps in and Jon immediately recognizes him. The driver slyly puts his finger to his mouth, signaling for Jon to be silent, and takes a seat opposite. Raul looks at the items on the table. "Dey have taken inventory of your t'ings?"

"Yes... Several times..."

"How are dey treatin' ya here, Mista Springa?"

"Fine, I guess... But, I've been here all night, and they haven't yet said what I'm charged with. *What's this about?*"

"I have been notified ta act as your attorney."

Jon turns to look at the observation mirror on the wall and then back at Raul. "You're an attorney?"

"Yes... Of course..."

"Do I *need* one?"

Raul coughs, leans on the table and lowers his voice. "You have been accused of possibly inciting insurrection and the attempted smuggling of high-value artwork."

"*Insurrection...?!*"

"Yes... Dey actually use dat one a lot ta keep enemies of da state from causing too much trouble."

"What about the *high-value artwork*?"

Raul shakes his head slightly and gives the subtle shushing motion again. "I will find out more ta what the specific charges are, but, in da meantime, sit tight and don't say anyt'ing t'incriminate yourself."

"I really don't know *anything*."

"That is best..." Raul stands and looks back to Jon's personal items on the table. "We will have ya outta dis place and on ya way home shortly."

"That would be nice..."

# Eric H. Heisner

When Raul gives a wave toward the big mirror and turns to the doorway, the door unlocks and opens for him to exit. "Don't go anywhere, until I get back."

Jon looks around the room. "Where would I *go?*"

The door slams closed and locks behind him. Left alone, Jon glances at the wall mirror, folds his arms across his chest, sits tight and waits.

~*~

On the coast of a Caribbean Island, the Key West Air Charters seaplane sits on a stretch of beach. Further inland, Rollie takes a nap in a hammock. Angie, in a skimpy bikini, holds a paper as she trots over from the beachside resort to give the hammock a shake. "Rollie... You awake?"

The pilot opens his eyes and gazes skyward. When she leans over him, he notices her revealing swim top and smiles. "I don't know... Maybe I'm dreaming." She jabs her knee into the underside of the hammock, and the pilot shifts with a grunt. "Okay... I'm awake *now.* What is it?"

Angie hands the note to Rollie. "This came for you."

He slowly scans the brief message and looks back at her. "Did you read this?"

"Yes."

"How did they even know where we were?"

"Coconut telegraph..."

Rollie grimaces at her remark and sighs. "Well, damn... What the hell are *we* supposed to do about it?"

She smiles sweetly. "We could rescue him again."

"What's *with* this guy?"

# Dominica Dash

At the thought of them not helping, Angie gets defensive and gives the hammock a shove. "It's *not* his *fault*."

"Yeah, I would say that the first few times, but…"

She cuts him off with a stern look and adds, "Jon was asked to do this as a special favor, and now *we're* being asked to do one for *him*."

"Uh, geez…"

"*C'mon*, Rollie…"

The pilot reads the note again and lies back into the slow swing of the hammock. "I guess we could hop over a few islands and be on the coast of Guadeloupe in a couple hours." He studies the instructions in the message. "Why don't we just pick him up in Dominica right now?"

"He's being informally detained for *suspicious activity*."

"Well, the people who got him *into* this are getting him out of there, aren't they?"

"Yes, they're working on it now, but do *you* want to be questioned by the authorities, too?"

The pilot glances at his seaplane pulled up on the beach. "No… No, I don't."

# XV

Stretched out in the chair, Jon stares at his things on the table. He looks at his watch again and shakes his head. Then, he hears the snap of the lock, and the door opens. "Finally…" The guard steps in and closes the door behind him. Puzzled, Jon leans his chair back on two legs. "What…? No visitors?" Moving closer, the guard laces his fingers together and cracks his knuckles. Standing before Jon, he peers down at the prisoner leaning back in the chair. Uncertain, Jon looks up at him, then over to the observation mirror and then back to the guard. "Hey, big guy, what's going on?" Without emotion, the guard balls his fist and smashes it down into Jon's face, knocking him off his chair.

In pain and shock, Jon glares at the officer. "Uh… Weren't you supposed to ask me a *question*?" Reaching down, the guard grips him by the shirt collar. He lifts Jon to his feet, stabilizes him briefly, and then punches him again. In agony, Jon crumples to the floor. He touches the side of his face, and puts up a hand to deflect, as the guard advances on him again. "Wait, wait... I've told them everything I know."

The guard lifts Jon from the floor and holds him steady. Jon covers his face, but this time the guard delivers a solid punch to his midsection.

~*~

The skies over Dominica darken, as black clouds, twist and swirl across the horizon. Heavy drops of rain begin to fall, and the warm breeze coming in from across the cool Atlantic steadily picks up.

~*~

Bleeding from his nose, Jon sits slumped in the chair with the guard positioned behind him. The smear of blood at their feet slowly darkens, as Jon stares downward and heaves a labored breath. Then, the door opens, Jon looks up, and the Chief Inspector enters.

The inspector takes a drink from a can of soda and sets it on the table. He finishes chewing something, as he pulls back the chair opposite Jon and takes a seat. "So, Mister Springer... What news might you have for me?"

Looking up through bruised and swollen eyes, Jon sees the man push the soda can aside, next to his belongings. "Sorry, I don't know what *any* of this is about."

With a displeased shake of his head, the inspector sucks food from his teeth and rubs them with his tongue. "Very disappointing... I thought you would be much smarter about this, and tell us what we need to know."

"If I *knew* what you wanted, I would *tell* you."

Leaning forward to put his elbows on the table, the inspector speaks frankly. "You see, we have a tiered system set up here, where you can invest in our country and, in return, receive certain benefits."

Jon stares at him and then glances at the guard standing close by. "Is *this* how you treat *tourists?*"

The inspector grins. "My apologies for the ill-treatment, but you are suspected of circumventing the process in an attempt to undermine our system."

"How long are you going to keep me?"

"That depends on how much your generous friend thinks you're worth."

"I'm being held for *ransom?*"

"No, no, no... That is such an *ugly* word. You are a person of special interest, being held until the proper *financial* arrangement can be made to secure your release."

Wincing in pain from his injuries, Jon raises an eyebrow. The inspector stares at Jon, takes the last sip of his soda and then nods to the guard. Suddenly, Jon is lifted from his seat by the nape of his neck and held over his chair. The Chief Inspector scoots his own chair back, stands away from the table and tersely declares, "Mister Springer, our patience in this matter is running low. You will provide us the information we desire, or there will be dire consequences."

As he glances back at the guard, Jon swallows hard and braces for another beating. "You're really putting a downer on my vacation. I won't have *anything* nice to say about *this* place."

# Dominica Dash

When the inspector groans and nods, the guard hauls back and smashes his fist into Jon's ribcage. The blow knocks the air from Jon's lungs and, when the guard releases his grip, Jon crumples to the floor in a heap. Through a haze of pain, he gasps for air, as he sees the shoes of the inspector and the guard step across the floor, stop as the door opens, and then exit. Alone in the silence of the room, a wave of anguish overwhelms Jon, and he passes out.

~*~

In a plush office with dark curtains back in Key West, Giselle, the owner of the Clipped Kitty, sits behind a large desk. She writes something down on a pad of paper, then turns to stare at the glowing screen of her computer. A chart of the Caribbean Sea, stretching from the Florida Keys to the Bahamas, all the way down to the windward islands of the Lesser Antilles, illuminates the dimly lit room.

After studying the map for a moment, she turns to pick up the handset of her desk phone. She dials a number, and waits patiently as it rings several times. When a voice answers, Giselle looks at her scribbled notes on the pad before stating, "This is C. K. Enterprises. I would like to transfer a large sum of money to an off-shore account."

The person affirms the request on the other end of the line and Giselle puts her finger to the numbers on the pad. "Yes... I have the account numbers. Are you ready?"

# XVI

Near his seaplane, Rollie stands at the water's edge and watches the ominous clouds forming to the south, until Angie comes out of the beach bungalow wearing a flowered cover-up. As she trots across the sand to join him, he turns to ask her, "What's the latest news on our writer friend?"

"They're making the arrangements."

Rollie gestures to the menacing skies. "This time of year, I don't like to see weather like that coming in."

She turns to look at the dark clouds. "I'll see what I can do to hurry things along…"

"If a tropical storm is blowing in, this rescue mission might have to be put on hold."

"Not much we can do about it… I'll let the flight center know we need the latest weather updates."

His gaze fixed on the clouds along the southern horizon, Rollie nods and murmurs, "Yeah… There's no trying to reason with hurricane season."

~*~

As someone gently touches his forehead, Jon wakes up. When his eyes open, he realizes that he is still on the cold floor of the interrogation room. His blurred vision slowly clears, and he recognizes the dark features of Raul, who asks, "How are ya, my friend?"

With a sigh, Jon groans, "Not great…"

"What happened?"

Jon rolls over, looks up to see the underside of the table and then looks over to see the big, two-way mirror on the wall. "I must have fallen."

Meekly, Raul smiles. "And hit several fists on da way…"

It hurts to laugh, so Jon tries not to. "I'm not sure how much more of this vacation I can stand. When are you going to get me out of here?" Raul turns to the mirror and waves someone in. The door creaks, and the guard with the experienced knuckles enters. Jon's eyes go wide at the sight of him, and he gasps, "I think I've had *enough* of *him*…!"

Raul notices Jon's alarm and pats him on the shoulder. "It's okay… He's assisting *us* now."

Jon winces. "*His* are the fists I fell *into repeatedly*…!"

The guard walks over to the table and carefully stuffs Jon's belongings into the backpack. Jon stares in utter disbelief, as Raul helps him to his feet. "Sorry about dat… But, since da last time we talked, da winds of loyalty have shifted."

Still unsteady, Jon needs Raul's help to stand. *"Shifted…?* What shifted them?"

*"Money…"* Raul whispers, so the guard won't hear him. "Not a *lot* of money, but it is a lot for *him*."

"From who…?"

Raul helps to steady Jon, as they move to the table. "Noth'n ta worry 'bout… It is *all* taken care of."

Unsure, Jon glares at the guard, who unexpectedly breaks into the friendliest of smiles. Pressing his tongue against the inside of his swollen cheek and tasting blood, Jon tries to shake off the painful experience. "So, am I getting out of here?"

Raul grabs Jon's bag from the guard and hands him his passport. "Yes…"

They all move to the doorway, and Raul peeks out before turning back to them. "All clear… Let's go."

Jon is just about to follow the driver out of the room, when there is a tentative cough from the guard behind them. Raul stops at the door and holds up his hand. "One last thing… Would you like to do the honors?"

Confused, Jon looks from Raul to the guard. "What…?"

Raul motions to the guard. "He needs ta have a reasonable excuse for ya departure."

The guard, with his feet braced shoulder-width apart, lifts his chin and points to it. Jon looks at Raul with surprise. "You want me to *hit* him?"

"He will have *much* trouble, if ya don't."

# Dominica Dash

With a welcoming grin, the guard presents his chin. *"Really...?"* Considering the lingering pain of his old-fashioned interrogation, Jon decides to comply. "Well... Okay then..." With the beating fresh in his mind, he reels back and swings. The roundhouse punch lands perfectly on target, snapping the guard's head to the side and tipping him back on his heels. Slowly, at first, like a tree being felled, the guard tips backward to land with a solid thud on the interrogation room floor.

Jon turns to Raul, who nods his approval. "Oh, very nice. And, on da first try, too!"

As they head out the doorway, Jon rubs his tingling fist and glances back at the unconscious guard. "A boxer friend in Key West showed me a few things..."

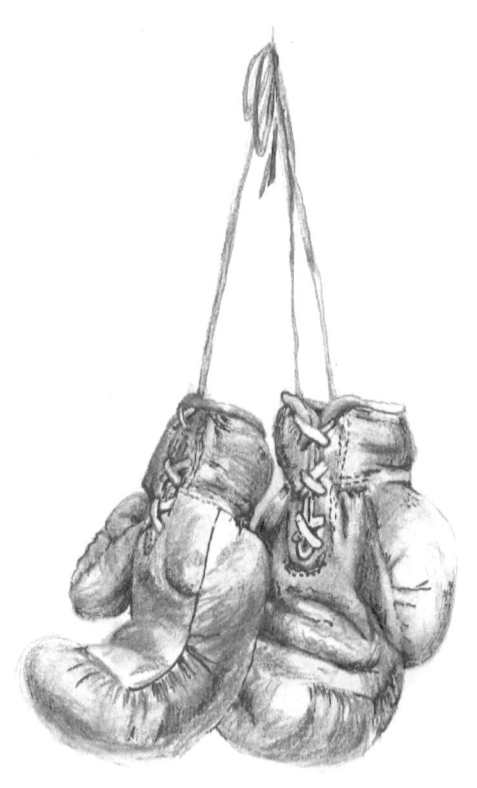

# XVII

Under the cover of a dark and stormy sky, Jon and Raul pop out through the back service door of the Ministry of Security, and they quickly trot across the parking lot to the airport shuttle van parked in the alleyway. Raul opens the front door for Jon. "Hurry, get in. We don't have much time before da emergency notice goes out on da police 'n da military radios."

"Dominica *military?* How *big* is it?"

"Large enough ta monitor da few roads on da island…"

As Jon gets into the van, Raul jogs around to get in the other side and sits behind the right-hand-side steering wheel. Confused, Jon stares at the glove compartment and mutters, "English… I can't get used to the driver being on that side."

The driver smiles and offers, "We try ta do t'ings *right*."

Raul starts the van, slams it into gear and drives down the alleyway. Gazing out the window at the weather, Jon slinks down in the passenger seat. "If they issue a search alert for me, how will I be able to get on a flight out of here?"

"First, we need ta get ya out of town, away from here and off da main roads."

Jon watches the concrete buildings of the city passing by. "How are we going to do that?"

"Have ya ever ridden a horse?"

Wide-eyed, Jon turns to see if his driver is joking with him, but Raul does not have even a hint of a jest on his face. "Well, I've seen a lot of Westerns…" With a gulp, Jon slinks further down in the seat, wondering how he manages to get himself into these situations.

~*~

The Chief Inspector and another officer stand in the doorway after discovering the guard laying on the floor in the middle of the interrogation room. The inspector goes over, taps the bottom of the guard's shoe with his foot and shakes his head when there is no response. "Damn…" To the officer standing by, he grumbles, "Put out a radio bulletin that we now have a *political fugitive*. We need to lock down *all* roads and ports. Land, sea, and air." The officer gives a nod and dashes off.

Surveying the room for anything left behind, the inspector steps over the guard and mutters, "Our special guest has just disproved his proclaimed innocence."

~*~

# Dominica Dash

Deep in the jungle, Raul's van drives up a twisted dirt lane as heavy clouds churn across the sky and block out the midday sun. Bumping and scraping through gaping potholes, they pass several mountain fields with grazing animals and overgrown fences. Finally, he pulls into a driveway that leads to a ramshackle dwelling with a lean-to outbuilding barn.

When the van pulls up, a middle-aged woman steps from the house. She looks to the sky, as a drop of rain splashes down from dark clouds, and a breeze sends a wave of leaves across the yard. Near the barn, Raul stops the van and gets out. "Hello, Marguerite... Meet our friend, Mista Jon Springa..."

On the other side of the van, Jon gets out and curiously looks the woman over. The first thing he notices is that she isn't wearing any shoes. Except for the pink paint on her toenails, her mud-crusted feet seem almost a part of the dirt driveway.

In a distinct English accent, she greets her company. "Hallo there, chaps. Looks like we'll be having a spit of rain, while we are doing a bit of horsey play."

Smiling at her British turn of a phrase, Jon grabs his backpack from the van. "Hello, Ms...?"

"You can call me Marguerite, or just *Marg* for the whole brevity thing, if you please."

"Okay... *Marguerite*..." Jon looks around the farmyard and sees only a few goats and sheep grazing in a far-off field. Then, he spots a small donkey and hopes that's not what she meant by *horsey-play*. Raul moves closer to Marguerite and whispers something in her ear. While looking at Jon, she nods, and he feels her eyes upon him. He asks, "What's the plan to transport me off the island?"

Raul turns to Jon. "We have ta git ya ta da nort' coast, where a boat can take ya from dere."

"How far is it?"

The driver shrugs. "We have but a small island here, which makes it a short distance. But, it is very difficult, since all da main roads will be cut off ta us." He gestures to the woman. "Marguerite will guide y'along da trails tonight."

As the sunlight fades behind the mountains, Jon looks to the stormy skies. "I'm riding the trails at night?"

Raul nods. "Wit' da storm comin', time is short."

Jon looks to the woman. "Is it *safe?*"

Flashing crooked, stereotypical British, tea-stained teeth, she jokes, "As long as you don't go and mosey off a cliff, it is."

"*Cliff…?*"

As he returns to the van, Raul explains, "Dere *are* some steep parts of da trail, but Marguerite can navigate dem wit' her eyes closed."

"But, *can the horse…?*"

The locals laughed off Jon's worried comment as a joke. But, Jon gets truly nervous, when Raul opens the driver's-side door and offers, "I will meet up wit' ya on da nort' coast."

As his trusted contact gets into the van to leave, Jon asks, "What about that special package I was supposed to deliver?"

A splash of rain falls, and Raul looks to the menacing clouds above. "It is *all* bein' taken care of."

# Dominica Dash

"By *who*...?"

Raul shuts the van door, opens the window and smiles. "See ya again very soon, Mista Jon Springa..."

Jon stares, dumbfounded, as Raul waves, turns the van around and drives off. He hitches his backpack up on his shoulder and walks over to join Marguerite. He glances down at her bare feet and notices the grime between her crusty toes. With a gulp, he asks, "When do we leave?"

"I'll get you saddled on Ol' Hurricane, and we'll be off."

He watches, as she unflinchingly walks the uneven path of stones to the barn. Looking to the dark sky, Jon takes a deep breath and mutters, "Yeah... *Ol' Hurricane* is *just* what I need."

# XVIII

Rollie helps Angie climb up to the nose hatch of the seaplane. He glances down the empty beach, then, with growing concern, looks out to the increasingly rough waters and at the stormy skies above. "If we don't get out of here soon, we'll get stuck here for the duration."

Angie wiggles down through the hatch compartment. "We are cleared to land at the airport in Guadeloupe."

"Fine… Let's get going."

She ducks down inside, and Rollie climbs to the hatch. He drops his feet into the opening, looks out to the rough ocean waters once more and murmurs, "Jon… You're either a real lucky fella, or one hell of a bad-luck charm." He slips down and pulls the hatch door closed behind him. In the cockpit, Angie rises from between the pair of pilot chairs and stands at the entry to the cargo hold. Meanwhile, Rollie crawls in from the hatch access point, gets situated behind the flight controls and puts on his headset.

~*~

Marguerite leads a single horse from a corral, behind the house, to the lean-to. Jon stands, mystified, as she ties off the shabby, mud-caked animal to the hitching rail. She brushes the horse down a bit and tosses an old, beat-up saddle on its back. Looking around for another animal, Jon goes over to talk to her. "Which one am *I* riding?"

Marguerite looks at Jon's swollen nose and bruised eye, then gives a chuckle. "How hard were you hit on the head?"

"Why...?"

"How many horses do you see here?"

"Just this one..."

"Well, that's it."

"Are we riding together? *Double...?*"

The crusty, old gal shimmies her hips suggestively and grins at Jon. "You wish, you cheeky bugger! I'm not falling for that ol' saddle-horn trick." Put off by the lewd sexual reference, Jon keeps quiet, as she finishes with the cinch strap and adjusts the length of the stirrups. She turns to him, grins that English smile and waves him up. "Hop aboard, laddie."

"What about you?"

"I'll hoof it along just fine."

Jon looks down at her dirty feet. "You're *kidding...*"

"Nope..."

"But, you don't have any shoes on."

She pats the horse on the shoulder and taps its hoof with a filthy toe. "Neither does he…"

"But… *Their* feet…"

Before he can finish his sentence, Marguerite lifts her dirt-crusted foot to show Jon the bottom. She taps it with her finger, as if it was the leather sole of a gentleman's dress shoe. "You see, I gots the blessing of hard feet."

Shrugging off the unpleasant sight of her grimy toenails, Jon turns away. "Yes, you certainly do…"

She gestures to the horse. "You know how to get on?"

"I rode once. At summer camp…"

"Well, *hop aboard*, camper!"

Jon slips his arms through his backpack straps, places a foot in a stirrup and climbs into the saddle. Gazing down at Marguerite, he asks, "Will you be able to keep up?"

Peering back at him, she flashes her tea-stained teeth. "Whoa there, Tom Mix… *I* know the way and you *don't*, so stick with *me*." She looks to the stormy skies. "It'll be dark soon. If you walk off the trail and die, you'll owe me a horse."

Jon stares at Marguerite, not knowing how to respond, as she turns and trots off. Eventually, he kicks his heels and steers the horse in her direction. "Let's go, horse. Giddy-up…"

# XIX

The jungled, mountainous interior of the island is dark and quiet. A warm wind blows through the trees, and raindrops occasionally shower down through the foliage. Jon can barely make out the ghostly figure jogging on the trail in front of him. He adjusts the shoulder straps of his backpack and settles in for the ride, as the horse seems to know what it's doing and where they are going.

When the moon peeks through the clouds with a silvery glow that penetrates the leafy canopy, the trail can be seen. Using moonlight, Jon studies his surroundings as best he can. He notices that the birds and insects are all quiet in anticipation of the coming storm. Briefly, as they move through a clearing, he can see out to the east shore of the island.

Ahead, Marguerite travels silently, except for the soft padding of her bare feet on the rocky trail. Suddenly, she stops and waits for Jon to catch up. He rides alongside her and pulls back on the reins. "What is it?"

"Shhh…"

They listen to the occasional gusts of wind blowing through the trees, until Marguerite finally pulls a plastic bottle from the saddlebag and takes a sip. Jon gazes down at her. "What did you hear?"

"Nothing… That's the problem…"

Jon looks up to see the moon break through some clouds, and remarks, "It's the middle of the night. What else is there?"

With an odd expression on her face, she looks at him and whispers, "There are a lot of jungle creatures that only come out in the night. They make a heck of a racket when *not* disturbed."

The moon gets blocked by clouds, and Jon scans through the darkness as he listens. "Maybe the storm has them quiet?"

"Yeah… That's probably what it is. I was just thinking, if they have all the main roads closed while searching for you, they might have soldiers posted on some of these trails, too."

"Makes sense… Is there any other way?"

"No… Not unless you can fly."

Jon holds the horse from walking off, while he looks down at Marguerite. "How did *you* become a part of this?"

She flashes her toothy grin in the night and whispers, "It's funny, because, initially, I got started here on the island through the foreign investment program.

My dumbass husband-at-the-time brought us here to start his business."

"Ranching...?"

She lets out a cackling laugh and then quiets herself. "Not hardly... I bought my little place *after* he disappeared."

"Disappeared?"

"He was arrested on international criminal charges and promptly extradited. He is in prison somewhere. Or, dead..."

"What kind of work did he do?"

In the darkness, he can see her turn away, as she mutters, "He was a crook."

Jon senses her reluctance to continue the conversation, so he sits waiting for Marguerite to proceed down the trail. Unhurried, she takes another sip from the plastic bottle and then offers it up to him. "Thanks..." He takes a big swallow, gasps, and then spits it out. "What the hell *is* that stuff?"

"Chocolate goat milk, with a little something extra..."

Spitting again, Jon tries to get the taste out of his mouth. "That's the *worst* chocolate milk I've *ever had!*"

"Just because it's not sugared-up and ice-cold like you Yanks like it..." She takes another swig and sighs with satisfaction. "Maybe, it's the local sugar cane liquor, or perhaps the cream-of-the-teat goat milk, that turns you off?"

"It's a very strange brew..."

The feisty woman does a deep squat and flexes her arms. "Keeps me strong!"

# Dominica Dash

Struggling to get rid of the awful taste, Jon sweeps his tongue around the inside of his mouth. "I'll stick with water."

"Did you bring any?"

"No."

She laughs and tucks the bottle back into the saddle bag. "Luckily, this island has hundreds of rivers and fresh springs. There is a nice one that comes right out of the mountain, ahead. We'll water the horse there, and you can wet your whistle."

She jogs off into the distance, and his horse follows her at a trot. Wiping the misty rain from his face, he rides off into the dark jungle, still spitting the horrid taste from his mouth.

# XX

Clomping along as the storm clouds intensify overhead, Jon soon finds himself in a clearing. Not able to see any sort of trail, Jon calls into the darkness. *"Marguerite…?!"*

The horse shakes its head, tugs on the bridle bit and goes over to a stone wall, where a stream of water flows from a crack in the rock. Not knowing where his trail guide went, Jon decides to stretch his legs and get some water, so he dismounts. Holding the reins in one hand, he cups his other under the trickling stream. As the horse sucks from the pool of water at the base of the rock, Jon takes a test sip. "Ahh… Cold water…"

As Jon drinks some more, a gruff voice unexpectedly erupts from the darkness. *"Who's out dere?!"* Jon stops drinking and stands motionless. When nothing else is said, he slowly turns to the sound of tactical boots tromping up the dark trail. A light clicks on, and its bright beam cuts through the night. "Don't move! Stay where y'are."

Behind the horse, Jon peeks over the seat of the saddle to see a soldier armed with a machine gun. When the flashlight shines in his direction, Jon ducks down and raises his hands. *"Don't shoot!!"*

"What are ya doin' out 'ere?"

"Just out for an evening ride..."

"It's late, and dere's a *storm* comin'."

Peeking over the saddle again, Jon squints into the beam of light as the soldier approaches. "Yeah... I figured I should get home."

"Where are ya comin' from?"

Jon pauses. "Yonder..."

The soldier shines his light at the edge of the clearing. "Step out from behind dat animal." With his hands raised, Jon uses the horse's reins to turn the animal away from the water. The soldier stares at them and then asks, "What's ya name?"

Before Jon can think of a good answer, there is a flash of movement from the jungle, followed by a banshee-like scream. Someone charges at the soldier and, before he can turn his flashlight to see, a tree limb smashes alongside the man's head and knocks his helmet off. With a groan, the soldier crumples into a heap on the ground.

The soldier's loose flashlight rolls across the clearing and shines into the underbrush. Jon squints to make out the shadowed figure watching for any other movement, as it looms over the soldier. Finally, Marguerite steps into the light and tosses her stick aside.

# Dominica Dash

Casually, she stares at Jon and queries, "Well, are you going get back on that horse or what?"

"Yes, ma'am!"

Jon tosses the reins over the horse's neck, puts a foot to the stirrup and mounts. He turns the horse around just in time to see Marguerite wave him on, as she jogs down the path in the direction the soldier came from. He urges the horse to a trot, catches up to her, then leans down and hisses, "Won't there be more of them this way?"

"Possibly... When that one comes around, he'll use the radio, and these trails will be thick with 'em, like flies on shit."

"What then...?"

"I hope to have you to the coast and on the boat by then." The woman runs on ahead, and Jon is amazed by the steady pace she keeps. A flash of lightning illuminates the narrow trail, followed shortly by a loud clap of thunder. When Marguerite, barely panting, glances back at him, she speaks in a low voice. "We'll stay off *all* the main trails now. I know a shortcut through the old fort. It can get right dodgy in bad weather, but I don't think we've had any big rains wash it out yet."

Clinging to the horse's mane, Jon trots along behind the woman. Unsure of how to respond to her, he puts on a false air of confidence. "If the *horse* can do it, surely *I* can."

Over her shoulder, she turns to smile at him, and she picks up her running pace. "Atta-boy, *John Wayne*!"

~*~

# Eric H. Heisner

Emergency lights flash at a military roadblock set up along the highway. Several Armed Forces vehicles standby, as police cars form a checkpoint. Uniformed officers, along with personnel in tactical gear, are positioned to search every vehicle that passes. People get out of their cars to assess the situation, and the traffic is lined-up for a mile in each direction.

# XXI

Unshod hooves clamor through the underbrush and slip on wet rocks, as the horse scrambles up a narrow, twisting path. Jon clings to the saddle, ducking under tree branches that scrape against his shoulders and pack. Suddenly, the moonlight reveals a castle-like stone structure in the midst of the jungle. The high-walled ruins of a Spanish fort…

When a flash of lighting further illuminates the deserted military compound, Jon takes in the magnitude of the site. Then, he notices Marguerite still jogging a short distance ahead. As she stops to wait for him, the rain starts to pour down in heavy sheets. When he catches up to her, he sweeps the water from his face and utters, "It's raining…"

"Oh… You noticed!"

# Dominica Dash

"How much farther…?"

"Not far…"

Another flash of lightning reveals a dark figure darting from the trailhead and ducking behind a tightly stacked wall of stones. Looking to Marguerite, Jon gasps, *"What was that?!"*

"Another one of them soldiers..." She waves Jon onward. "Get out of here! Follow the path down to the coast! *Go, go…!!"* After pointing Jon to the trail, Marguerite jumps to the side, over a low, broken wall. But, before he can kick-start the horse, he hears the all-too-familiar click of an automatic rifle.

"Hold it right where y'are!"

Through flashes of lightning and pouring rain, Jon can just barely make out two soldiers stepping from the fort ruins. As they advance on him, he lifts his hands high in surrender. "Uh… Hello…?"

*"You* on da *horse.* Keep ya' *hands up!"*

Instead, Jon leans down, wraps his arms around the horse's neck and whispers, "I don't think she has a club big enough for the both of them. Let's not stick around to find out." As the soldiers approach, Jon marks their position by the glow of their night vision goggles. When they are almost upon him, Jon smacks his heels into the horse's belly, and the animal rears up, kicking out its front feet.

Several bolts of lightning suddenly flash across the sky, and the terrified soldiers jump back. Thunder rolls, as the horse's front legs come down and hit the ground running. Momentarily blinded by the lightning, the soldiers shoulder their weapons, but Jon has already galloped down the dark, jungle trail. They fire their guns, and bullets cut through the foliage and ricochet through the ruins.

Rain pours, the wind howls, and lightning flashes across the sky, as Jon's horse races through the trees. For a moment, he thinks he hears the distant popping of gunfire, but he keeps his attention ahead and doesn't look back. *"Holy crap, horse…!!!* I hope you know where we're *going…"*

As the horse makes a sharp turn around a corner, it's hooves slip on the mud-slicked trail. The animal slows a bit, then picks up the galloping pace on the straightaway. Terrified, Jon laments, while he holds on for his life. "I don't remember the movie-cowboys having to ride like this at night. Downhill… *In the rain…!"*

The horse charges down a trail revealed by occasional flashes of lightning. Jon clenches a handful of reins above the withers with all his might, as branches whip past his face. Finally, the trail opens to a rocky coastline under stormy skies. Pulling hard on the reins, Jon attempts to keep the animal from careening over a cliff. "Whooa, boy… *Whoaaa…!"* Down below, rough seas frame a trail along the beach, and Jon steers the horse toward it. A sliver of moonlight peeks through the clouds to show them the way. Jon turns to the mountainous terrain behind him, but he can no longer make out the old fort or the trail they just travelled. "Now, *where to…?"*

Slowing the horse's pace, Jon walks it down the beach, until he sees the faint outline of a person and possibly a boat. The beam from a flashlight blinks on, then suddenly cuts off. Unsure if it is a welcome signal or soldiers waiting for him, Jon checks over his shoulder. Seeing nothing but waves and pouring rain, he suggests, "Only one way to find out…"

# XXII

While Jon peers into the darkness, he urges the horse to plod forward through the soft, wet sand. They gradually move closer to the waterline, where, under the lapping waves, the sand is firmer. Swirling storm clouds overhead block the moonlight, as the wind blows continuous sheets of rain at them. The flashlight turns on again, and Jon heads toward it. "Hello…! Who's there?"

The beam of light clicks off, then unexpectedly clicks on pointed directly at Jon and the horse. Jon tugs back on the reins and braces himself to flee. Just as he is about to turn and run, he hears a familiar voice call, "Mista Springa…? Shielding his eyes from the glare of the light, Jon tries to identify who it is. The light clicks off, and the voice continues. "It's me.  Cap'n Ice. I come ta take ya 'way from 'ere."

Tapping the horse's side, Jon moves forward to see the boat captain standing next to the hotel's driver. He steps down from the horse. "Hello, Ice… Raul…? How did you get here?"

Despite the rain splashing across his face, Raul smiles. "Da blockades of all da roadways are only ta search for da Gringo Americano dey lost. I am not what dey're lookin' for."

When the driver, holding a wrapped package at his side, steps up to take the reins of the horse, Jon notices and points to the parcel. "What's that?"

"Dis was planned to be a much more casual exchange." He shrugs and holds the securely wrapped bundle out to Jon. "And, a lot less wet…"

Jon takes the flat, medium-sized package and weighs it in his hands. "Is this the artwork I was supposed to pick up?"

"Yes… It is now wrapped safely for ya boat ride."

Turning to the rough waves splashing along the coast, Jon then considers the small outboard watercraft before them. He turns to Ice and asks, "This is the boat we're going in?"

"It is da only boat dat I have."

"Can't we find a bigger one?"

Raul ushers Jon along. "It's da only one available ta us."

Jon peers through the darkness at his wristwatch, barely able to make out that it's almost four in the morning. He shakes his head and takes a step away from the water. "No, thanks… I've had some bad experiences with small boats."

# Dominica Dash

Raul and Ice exchange worried looks and urge Jon toward the vessel. "If we don't get ya out soon, we might have a hard time hidin' ya durin' da hurricane."

Jon sputters, *"There's a hurricane coming?!"*

Ice gets into the boat and waves for Jon to get aboard. "Dey say da bad stuff should be hittin' midday tomorrow."

Jon looks out to the dark, stormy skies and rough water. "How far to where we're going?"

Waves splash against Raul's knees, as he pulls Jon forward. "Da next island is only a few hours..."

Jon gestures to the outboard motor on the wooden boat. "The *next* island...? A *few hours* in *this thing?*"

Ice adjusts the choke, starts it, and throttles the engine up. "If we go now, before it gets worse, it might be do-able."

"Before it gets *worse...?!?*"

After pushing Jon aboard, Raul grabs the bow, ready to shove them off. "In a few hours, *no* size boat will be safe out dere in da heavy chop."

Tossing a salute toward Raul, the captain revs the small outboard engine. "I get ya dere, quick as I can."

Thigh-deep in the splashing water, Raul pats Jon's arm. "We don't have many options available. Dis is da best we can do for ya at dis time."

Shaking his head, Jon takes a seat in the rocking boat. "There doesn't seem to be any good way out of this." Tucking the package safely under his arm, he looks at the horse standing on the beach in the pouring rain. "What about Marguerite?"

# Eric H. Heisner

Pushing them away, Raul says, "I will hold da horse for her ta collect when she gets 'ere."

"She might've had a run-in with some soldiers at the old fort."

The driver smiles. "I'd be sorry for *dem!*"

The engine sputters a bit as Ice pushes-off with a paddle. He motions to Jon to situate himself under the canvas awning. "Hold tight! Time for us ta go, if we're ta make it."

Partially protected from the pouring rain, Jon tucks the wrapped artwork beneath his seat and then calls out to Raul. "When I get to the next island, *where do I go?*"

A bolt of lightning flashes, as Raul hollers back. "Jest go to da airport on Guadeloupe, 'n ya will meet wit' da…" The rest of what he says is covered by a booming clap of thunder. Standing with the horse, Raul watches them head out.

The boat turns into the churning waves and motors off. Jon sees Marguerite emerge from the jungle to join Raul and the horse on the beach. In the pouring rain, they both raise their hands to wave, and Jon returns the gesture.

Turning ahead, Jon sees only the nighttime glimmer of choppy waves. Holding onto his seat, he yells to the captain. "Do you think we can make it?"

With a firm grip on the rudder, Ice slings back his mop of wet hair and flashes a toothy grin. "A boat in harbor is safe, but dat's *not* what dey are *made* for."

# XXIII

Out on the open water, blowing rain stings the skin like a thousand needles. The ashore boat smashes through the chop, as water crashes over the bow, rocking them into the trough between swells, only to do it all over again. Eventually, the stormy, night sky gives way to a gloomy, gray morning.

Jon holds onto the package, while he clings to the bench. Over the noise of the motor, pouring rain, and waves splashing against the hull, Ice yells forward to him. "Ya might want ta grab hold of a lifejacket 'nstead of dat art!" Roused from his thoughts, Jon turns to the boat captain with a questioning stare, as Ice points to the dark, swirling clouds looming ahead. "We're headin' inta some bad stuff."

Jon looks to where Ice is pointing and sees storm clouds, full of lightning and torrential showers, bearing down on them. He pivots to look at Ice and hollers, "We're heading into *that?!*"

"Da island of Guadeloupe is *dat* a'way."

A rogue wave smashes against the port side of the boat and water cascades over the unfortunate men. Wiping the saltwater from his face, Jon questioningly looks to the captain. "What if this boat can't make it?"

"Den, we will have ta swim..."

Jon looks around the small, ocean-tossed watercraft. "Okay, I'll take a lifejacket now..." Ice points to a latched cabinet at the bow, and Jon cautiously makes his way forward. He opens the compartment and pulls out an orange life vest. Tucking the artwork into the cabinet, he puts the floatation device on and then turns to offer one to Ice. The captain smiles, declines with a wave, and pulls one out from under his seat.

After retrieving the art from the cubby and latching the door, Jon makes his way to his seat. As Ice maneuvers the boat through the choppy waters, another smashing wave hits their starboard side, and the splash knocks the wrapped package from Jon's grip. Before it washes overboard, he frantically grabs it back again. Then, he holds it tight against his life vest and stares directly at the rough waters ahead. Jon watches the pointed bow crash into one wave after another, as the boat drives straight into the rising swells in order to keep from being rocked broadside and capsizing.

For hours, the tiny boat motors through the ocean chop, gunning the engine up one side of a wave, cresting, and then sliding down the other. As the craft charges up another wall of water, the men see a larger vessel scanning through the haze with a searchlight. The bright lamp pans all around, but only catches stormy skies and blowing rain. Hastily, Ice cuts the engine and ducks down.

Jon looks back to the captain, as the boat, now at the mercy of the waves, bobbles without direction. "I saw a boat! Who were they?"

"Patrol boat…"

"From where…?"

"Most likely come from Dominica."

Jon bends low to keep out of view, and hears splashing around them, absent the motor. "How do you know?"

"Who else be dumb 'nough to be here in dis wea'der?"

As they crest another wave, Jon peeks over the side of the boat and then looks at Ice. "I was thinking the same thing!!!" A wave spins the boat sideways and water crashes over the rails, almost overturning the craft. Ice is nearly washed overboard, but he shakes it off, takes his seat again and starts the motor. Jon looks at the distant patrol boat and calls to Ice. "What are you doing…?"

"I need ta power dis boat head-on, or da waves will topple us next time."

The motor chugs to life, and Ice turns the boat to smash directly into the swells again. Jon's teeth rattle with the slamming jolt, and he yells, "Won't they hear us?"

"I'd radder dey hear our tiny motor dan *not* hear our calls for help from in da water."

Keeping low, Jon holds on, as the beaming searchlight passes over their heads just before they crest the next wave. Moments later, after blasting through another swell, they look around to see only rainy skies and choppy water. Before they dip between swells again, Jon pivots to scan the horizon. "Where did they go?"

"Da ocean gives and takes…"

"A boat *that* size…?"

"Who knows… Maybe dey's smart 'n head'n back home, or maybe dey's out dere swimmin' for deir life."

"What about us?"

Ice shivers in his life vest, sweeps the rain from his face and puts on his best grin. "Dey are like a toy boat in da bat'tub. *We* ride da waves like *a cork!*"

Confused, Jon looks at him. "So…?"

"You ever see one dat didn't take on water and sink?"

The cold realization of their situation hits hard, and Jon thinks about the danger. He holds tight to the seat in the boat, looks out to the dawning sky, and hopes he will get the chance to enjoy another day. Aching and sore from bracing himself, Jon looks to the package in his arms and hollers to the captain. "How much longer…?"

"Another hour or so…"

"*What?!?*"

"I've made dis trip in t'ree hours once, but it was pretty smood sailin'. Dis, not so much…"

Ice points ahead through the clouds to an outline of land. "Luckily, we can see it from 'ere."

Barely able to make out the landmass through the haze, Jon wonders, "When it was dark, how did you steer?"

# Dominica Dash

"I would've used da starry skies, if any were ta be seen. N'er know in a storm… But, da wind is steady, so I kept it off my shoulder 'n hoped for da best."

"*Hoped for the best?!?*"

"Island life down 'ere can blow ya in many directions. Ya cannot control it, but ya can work wit what it sends."

The boat rides up a swell, peaks out, and crashes down. Soaking wet, Jon sighs, "I don't see how that applies to us."

"Da life works out da way it will."

"So, you're saying we'll make it?"

"Possibly… Or, maybe not…"

Not reassured, Jon braces the package between his knees and pulls the straps of his life vest tighter. He looks out to the water raging all around them, and then he turns his focus to the faint image of land on the horizon.

# XXIV

The cloud-filled skies ahead of them are brighter than behind, but the ocean swells are just as choppy. Exhausted and seasick, Jon braces himself for the next jarring wave. Though they are gradually getting closer to the shore, Jon doubts that, in his exhausted condition, he could swim the distance. He looks at the package in his water-shriveled fingers and shakes his head. Softly, he mutters, "Should've known better than to think there's *ever* a free ride..." As Ice guns the motor to charge up another big swell, Jon shoves the package under his seat.

The captain calls, "We be in da home stretch now!"

~*~

Rollie paces a hallway at Pointe-á-Pitre International Airport on Guadeloupe Island. Holding a steaming cup of coffee, he stares at the weather forecast displayed on the television. When he notices Angie finishing with a payphone, he glances at his watch. "Any word from him?"

"They said the boat left six hours ago."

The pilot looks back to the updated storm report and shakes his head. "Even if we *could* fly out there to look for them, we couldn't land in these high seas."

Angie looks hopeful. "Maybe, they already made it ashore?"

"To where...? *South America...?*"

Outside, wind-battered trees bend, nearly breaking, and sheets of rain blow across the tarmac. As Angie watches through a plate-glass window, she notes, "Well, waiting around *here* isn't doing us any good."

Rollie points to the televised forecast. "If that tropical storm turns north, it will sweep over these islands and wipe out everything in its path. We need to be able to leave here at a moment's notice. Preferably, sooner..."

She looks outside to a line of taxicabs sitting at the curb in the pouring rain. "I'll take a taxi down the coast road and try to find out if any boats came in."

Shaking his head, Rollie states, "If this gets any worse, I'm leaving. No insurance will cover my ass if I stay here."

Angie shrugs dismissively and looks outside to the storm. "You gotta do what you gotta do... If it comes to that, I'll hunker down and catch the first commercial flight back to Key West."

"I don't want to just leave you here."

Heading toward the door and the waiting line of taxis, Angie turns back to Rollie. "Then, *don't...!*"

~*~

Ice steers the boat to the shore of Guadeloupe Island. Both of them appear worn-out and completely water-logged. Deep water sloshes back and forth at the bottom of the boat, washing over their already-soaked feet. As they near the shore, Ice motions for Jon to hop out. "Dis is your stop."

Jon turns to the captain. "Where…?"

"Here."

Scanning the empty coastline and the huge waves crashing on the beach, Jon wonders if there might have been a dock here before the storm. "There's nothing here…"

Ice points to a distant roadway above a jungled hillside. "D'airport is along dat road."

"Which way…?"

Ice scans the beach to get his bearings and then shrugs. "One way or da odder…" Continuously jolted by the swells, Jon is in no condition to argue about getting out. Near the shore, the waves crash down with a thunderous roar, as strong undercurrents pull back from the beach. Gunning the engine, Ice hollers and points landward. "Ya have ta get out 'n swim!"

Jon turns to stare at him. "*Swim?!?*"

As they bob between cresting waves, Ice maneuvers the craft in an attempt to keep them from capsizing. He yells, "Can't get any closer to da beach, or I smash on da big rocks." Jon looks appalled, and Ice laughs. "No worries…! Ya won't get more wet dan ya a'ready are!"

Jon peers over the side at the choppy water crashing on the beach. "*Rocks…?*" Shaking his head, he moves to the bow, preparing to jump overboard. Before he gets up the nerve, he hears Ice call, "Hey dere, Springa... Don't forget ya t'ing."

Ice grabs the wrapped artwork from the underside of the bench seat and holds it out to Jon. Suddenly, a surging wave lifts the back end of the boat up, until they are nearly vertical. As Jon gawks at the boatman, the watercraft topples, end over end, and Ice is catapulted from the stern into the raging sea. Tossed from the boat, the last things Jon sees are big rocks, churning water and a life vest washing past him.

# XXV

From inside a taxicab, Angie struggles to see the coastline through sheets of pouring rain. She taps the driver on the shoulder and motions for him to stop the car. "Pull over…"

"Again…?"

The driver stops at the side of the road, and Angie steps into the downpour to scan the coastline on the other side of the highway. She peers into the gloom, and, as dark clouds twist and turn, her jaw clenches with worry. The cab driver leans over, opens the passenger-side window a crack and shouts, "Missus, if your friend is out dere boating in dis bad weather, methinks 'e is in *big trouble*."

Angie glances back to the taxi. "Yeah…"

Sweeping back her wet hair, she scans the area once more and then climbs back into the cab. The driver turns to see her dripping on his seat. "Ya need a towel. Wanna keep goin' ?"

"Let's go another mile or two."

"Okay, boss-lady…Ya're payin' da fare."

~*~

Surrounded by activity and bright lights, Jon wakes up in a hospital room. He finds himself dressed in a gown, and, when he tries to move his arm, he discovers that handcuffs secure his wrist to the bed. Sitting up, he looks out the window and sees dark clouds and heavy rain. He yanks the handcuffs against the bed rail and accidentally clicks them tighter. "Dammit… How the heck did I get *here?*"

Seeing a uniformed security guard nearby, he asks, in his best Spanish, "Hola… Donde estoy y como… Aqui?"

With distain, he looks at Jon and answers in French. "Vous êstes arrivé ici dans des circonstances suspectes."

"*What…?*" Dumbfounded, Jon looks around the hospital room and notices that the signboards are written in French. "Am I on Guadeloupe Island?"

"Oui."

Understanding *yes*, but none of the prior reply, Jon lies back in the bed. He observes that the hospital is being prepped for an emergency weather event. As people pass by, most divert their eyes, but, occasionally, someone sneaks a peek in his direction. Staring up at the ceiling panels, he gives a tug of his handcuffed wrist and murmurs, "At least I'm not on that boat… Or, in the interrogation room…"

# Dominica Dash

~*~

Wind blows heavy sheets of rain across the runway. Inside the terminal, Rollie looks outside at his idle seaplane. After glancing at his watch again, he looks back to the televised warning of a severe hurricane. Grumbling to himself, he huffs, "C'mon, Angie… I gotta go…" As clouds twist menacingly across the sky, he shakes his head, upset. "I'm sorry, Darlin'. Can't stay here any longer…" Rollie charges out into the rain, takes cover under the high wing, then climbs through the rear hatch and into the cargo hold.

~*~

On the beach, Angie and a local woman stand talking in the rain. Their voices can't be heard through the blowing storm, but the lady pantomimes a boat coming in and then flipping. Angie looks down toward the end of the beach and questions her about where the boat went afterwards. The woman points out to sea and then points down the road in the other direction.

Understanding, Angie nods her head and gently touches the woman on the arm to express her thanks. She turns, runs back to the taxicab and climbs inside. The driver grimaces, as Angie, soaking wet, pushes back her hair and drips all over his back seat again. Leaning forward, she blurts, "The hospital… Take me to the nearest hospital, please!"

"If dat's where 'e is now, 'e's lucky it ain't da morgue." With windshield wipers flapping at high speed, the driver shifts into gear, pulls onto the pavement and splashes away.

# XXVI

The Grumman seaplane rumbles over to position itself on the runway and points its nose to the horizon. Engines throttle up, propellers whirl, and the high-winged, amphibious airplane rolls forward. Gradually picking up speed, the flying boat lifts into the air, its retractable wheels tucking back against the hull, as it soars up into dark, stormy skies.

~*~

Jon, exhausted after his open-water ordeal, naps with his cuffed wrist dangling from the bedrail. He hears a familiar voice whispering in his ear. "Jon... Wake up."

Shaken awake, Jon opens his eyes, blinks a few times to adjust to the bright lights and focuses on his friend's face. "Angie... Is that you?"

She smiles. "I need to stop finding you like this."

Jon lifts his cuffed wrist. "You mean, *handcuffed?*"

She plops his soaked backpack at the foot of the bed. "No... *Half-drowned...*"

"How did you find me?"

"It wasn't easy."

"Sorry..."

"Don't worry about it. Let's get you out of here."

Jon looks at his backpack and grimaces. Then, he tugs at his cuffed wrist and looks down at the flimsy hospital gown he's wearing. "How are we supposed to do that?"

After glancing around the crowded room to see if anyone is watching them, Angie inspects the cuffs. "These beds weren't designed to be jail cells." She puts her knee to the edge of the bed and tugs on the metal rail, until the plastic bracket at one end finally snaps. She smiles at Jon, as she slides the loose end of the handcuffs off the end of the rail. "*Anything* will break if you try *hard* enough."

With the handcuffs dangling from his wrist, Jon asks, "What about the part that's attached to *me?*"

"That'll have to wait. Your stuff is sopping wet, so I found some other clothes for you down the hall..." Jon sits up, swings his legs over and stands, as Angie gestures to a pile of folded items on the bedside chair. "Get dressed."

While the hospital staff busily prepare for the storm, Jon looks around. "What about the guard that was here?"

"He's on an extended coffee break."

Looking at Angie curiously, Jon asks, "Did you have to pay him off? Like the guard in Dominica...?"

# Dominica Dash

She smiles innocently. "It all goes on the tab of your special lady-friend, Jeanee' Renee'."

"*She* sent you?"

"The *least* she could do after getting you *into* this mess."

Jon slips into some baggy, reggae-style pants and then trades the hospital gown for a tie-dye t-shirt with the message: **I went to Jamaica... Got stoned, and all I got was this shirt**. He glances at the image of a fat marijuana joint on the front of it and looks back at Angie. "Whose clothes are these?"

"Some passed-out guy down the hall who looked to be about your size..."

"It looks like I'm wearing a Halloween costume."

She grins and waves him along. "Goes with the bracelet. C'mon... Get your stuff, and let's go..."

With the storm raging outside, no one pays any attention, as Jon grabs his backpack. Following Angie, he heads out of the room and down the hall. The security guard returns with a cup of steaming coffee, and Angie walks right past him. He gives her a cheerful smile and doesn't even glance at Jon.

Catching up to her, Jon whispers, "How much did you have to pay him?"

"Just enough..."

"He seemed very happy about it."

Angie leads Jon outside to a taxicab waiting at the curb. "Nobody really knew what to do with you during a hurricane, so they'll be glad to have you gone."

Jon looks back to the busy hospital and then out to the stormy skies. "*I'll* be glad to be gone."

They slip into the taxi, and the driver looks at Jon's outfit before rolling his eyes at the sight of the wet bag on his seat. Turning to Angie, he asks, "Ya be wantin' ta start a *new* fare, or just ta keep da *old* tab goin'?"

"Keep the clock rolling. To the airport, on the quick...!"

The driver glances at Jon again, this time noticing the dangling handcuffs. With a nod, he shifts the car into gear, leans forward to see beyond the flapping windshield wipers, then presses on the gas and drives off through the pouring rain. "Yeah, boss-lady...Ya're payin' da bill."

GUADELOUPE

DOMINICA

*Lesser Antilles*

MARTINIQUE

SAINT LUCIA

SAINT VINCENT & THE GRENADINES

# XXVII

After being dropped off in front of the airport, Jon follows Angie to where the planes are parked. Near the pilot entrance, she stares outside through the downpour, until Jon finally asks, "Where's Rollie?"

She murmurs, "He's gone…"

Not hearing her, he states, "I don't see the plane."

With a look of utter disappointment, Angie turns to Jon. "Crap… I didn't think he'd leave." On the wall behind them, a television set shows a map of the islands overlayed with a swirling path of inclement weather. She looks outside again and grumbles, "He really *did* fly off without us…"

"Maybe he left a note or something."

"No, I doubt it. I told him to go and take off if he had to, and that I'd find my own way home."

# Dominica Dash

As they stand at the doorway, splashes of rain blow in. Jon puts a hand to Angie's shoulder and takes a step back. "From the look of this weather, it's a good thing he's *not* here."

He ushers her inside, just as a gust of wind slams the door shut. Back in the lobby, Angie glances at the forecast on the TV and mutters to herself. "Rollie... I *can't* believe you actually left without me."

At the observation window, Jon looks out at the driving rain blowing across the runway. Concerned, he glances back at Angie and asks, "What now...?"

She sits in a lounge chair and combs her fingers through her hair. "Ah, let me think a minute. I was so set on finding you, that I didn't think beyond this storm. Or, that Rollie would leave us..."

While strong, gusting winds cause the airport windows to tremble, Jon thinks he hears the distant rumble of engines. After all his rescues and misadventures, Jon recognizes the distinct sound of the seaplane. Rubbing his forehead, he says, "I need some rest. Now, I'm hearing things."

Angie sits for a moment with her head in her hands. Then, she looks up at Jon questioningly. She listens and then gets up to join him by the window. "What did you hear? Probably just thunder..."

He presses his face to the window and strains to see through the pouring rain. "I thought I heard Rollie's seaplane."

Suddenly, Angie's features brighten, and she runs to the door and pushes it open. Rain blows in, as she steps outside to look up into the sky. "I think I hear it, too!"

Joining her in the downpour, Jon stares up to the dark, swirling clouds glowing with flashes of lightning. Following a rumble of thunder, the Grumman seaplane roars overhead and comes around for a landing. Jon and Angie watch with glee, as the amphibious aircraft touches down on extended wheels, turns, and taxis toward them.

Angie exclaims, "He came *back* for us!"

Through the gusting rain, the flying boat rolls up to the General Aviation hangar, brakes with one wheel and sweeps the tail end around broadside. The pilot window slides open, and Rollie pops his head out. "Why are ya out there standing in the rain? Get yer asses in here!"

With beaming smiles, Jon and Angie trot over to the plane, as the rear hatch door is opened and a short set of stairs is hung out from the lower rim. Rollie reaches out to help Angie climb inside and then grabs Jon's backpack as it is handed up. With a broad grin, he greets Jon. "Good to see you again, pal."

"Thanks for coming back for us."

He shrugs and wipes his wet hands. "Don't I always...?" While helping Jon into the plane, Rollie notices the dangling handcuffs. "Nice jewelry..."

Innocently, Jon lifts his shackled wrist and sighs. "I don't know *how* I get myself *into* these things."

"Getting *into* cuffs ain't hard; it's getting *out* of them that's the trick. I know someone that might be able to help."

"Why am I not surprised?"

Rollie pulls the stairway up and swings the hatch door closed. "With your crazy luck, *anything* is possible."

# Dominica Dash

Making his return to the front of the plane, he sees that Angie is already in the copilot seat. He grins at her, and then he looks back to the cargo area where Jon is. "All aboard?"

Turning from watching the raging weather, Angie looks at Rollie, as he puts on his headset and begins his preflight. "Thanks for coming back for us."

"I couldn't abandon you to some commercial flight. Those things are dangerous... You know, if they clear us for takeoff, we'll be heading home through some rough weather."

"Can we get *ahead* of the storm?"

"Maybe... It's working its way north. If we get above it, we have a chance to make it. When we stop to refuel in the Bahamas, we can reassess our situation."

Rollie adjusts his headset microphone and responds to a radio communication. To Jon's surprise, he even tosses in a few French words. From the cockpit threshold, Jon peeks over the pilot's shoulder and comments, "*You* speak *French?*"

"Only when I have to."

Rollie reaches overhead and adjusts the throttles to bring the plane around to the runway. Angie puts on her headset, looks back at Jon, and chimes in. "He can't order you anything fancy at a French restaurant, but he can make his way around an international airport."

Rollie grins and glances at her. "French fries for the lady, and a stack of French toast for me." She rolls her eyes at him, as the seaplane begins to roll forward onto the flooded runway. Rollie looks back at Jon and nods toward the back cargo hold. "Better have a seat and strap in. It's going to be a bumpy ride."

Jon flashes back to his overnight boat ride. "Ok, great... I was seasick this morning. might as well get airsick, too."

The pilot points to a plastic bag tucked in the seat pouch. "If yer gonna hurl, use the barf bag."

Rollie pushes forward on the throttles, releases the brake on the wheels, and the aircraft races down the runway. As the plane gains speed and lifts into the air, the rainwater streaking across the windows makes it hard to see outside. With its dual radial engines roaring, the seaplane lifts into stormy skies over the island of Guadeloupe and banks to the north.

# XXVIII

The Grumman seaplane plows through turbulent weather, constantly being lifted and tossed by forceful gusts of wind. Engines roaring, the plane flies higher to get above the storm. With ominous clouds all around, they push north.

Several hours later, through the torrential downpour, the seaplane makes an airstrip landing on an island in the Bahamas. A man in a yellow rain slicker and a rubber fisherman's hat waves, as he tows a fuel wagon over to them. Jon and Angie watch out the window, as the man sets up a ladder and begins to refuel the plane.

His earphones removed, Rollie lays his head back and quickly dozes off for a combat nap. His eyes pop open, when the man in the slicker hammers a fist on the hull of the plane to indicate that the tanks are filled. Rollie moves from his seat, scoots to the back of the plane, and opens the rear hatch to give payment to the attendant.

While returning to the cockpit, Rollie passes Jon, pats him on the arm, and hands him a vomit bag. "If you thought the last few hours were fun, you're gonna love what's ahead." He slips into his seat and fastens his lap belt. With concern, he looks over at Angie and then behind to Jon. "Jo-jo, out there, says the weather looks to be sweeping north faster than predicted. We were barely able to stay above it before."

Angie holds her headset in her lap. "What's the plan?"

"From here on, we'll go low, and see if we can skip along the whitecaps all the way home."

Jon leans forward and asks, "Maybe we should hold up here until the storm passes?"

Rollie glances at Jon's handcuffs and shakes his head. "No good... We'd have to clear customs to stay. We just got you out of a bind, and now you want to get into trouble again. They'd have questions about your dope outfit, not to mention your fancy bracelet." The pilot smiles. "Shouldn't be a huge problem getting home through this weather. Besides, we're in a flying boat." Not comforted by the ditching at sea joke, Jon clutches the vomit bag in his lap, looks at the flotation vests, and tugs his seatbelt tighter. He watches Rollie begin his usual preflight in preparation for departure.

The high-wing's dual engines roar to life, and the seaplane pivots on the starboard wheel, coming around to face the airstrip. Cleared for takeoff, the aircraft rolls forward through the onslaught of rain. They're the only activity on the runway, as they pick up speed and splash through puddles, before they take to the air. Briefly touching down once and then lifting to the sky, the airplane flies into the ominous weather of the approaching hurricane.

~*~

The gusting winds are stronger now. Low on the deck, the seaplane charges ahead over choppy waters. Tentatively, Jon makes his way up to the cockpit and pokes his head in. "How're we doin'?" Holding onto the bulkhead as the plane jolts, he asks, "Are we almost out of this weather?"

With a chart spread across her lap, Angie feigns a smile. Rollie keeps both hands firmly on the yoke, as he muscles the aircraft through the turbulent skies. He nods to his nervous passenger without glancing back. "We'll make it. I think…"

Jon braces himself, as he fends off a wave of nausea. "Uh… I haven't seen signs of land for quite a while."

White-knuckling the controls, Rollie responds calmly. "No more island hopping… We're gonna cut across open water and hope to get to Key West before the hurricane does."

Jon sputters, "Is this an *actual* hurricane?"

Forceful winds shift the plane sideways, and Jon hangs on as Angie inadvertently bumps her head on the side window. She adjusts her headset. "Yeah… They just upgraded it to a category three, and it's moving northwest toward the Gulf."

# Eric H. Heisner

Rollie rights the wings to bring them back on course, and he hollers back to Jon, "With it giving us a hell of a tailwind, we're making good time. But, it's really nipping at our heels." Rollie clings to the yoke, as the airplane jolts violently again. "You'd better sit down and buckle-in. This is gonna get a helluva lot worse!" He peers back at Jon. "You better slip one of those *PFDs* on, just in case."

"In case of what...?"

Grimly, Rollie stares forward. "In case we have to ditch."

Jon looks into the cargo hold. "What's a *PFD?*"

Angie clarifies. *"Personal Floatation Device..."*

After releasing his grip on the bulkhead, Jon staggers to his seat and is just about to sit when the airplane shakes violently. Nearly missing his chair, he steadies himself and then quickly sinks into his seat. He buckles himself in and looks to the life vests fastened on the wall. From the cockpit, Rollie yells, "Just like our motto promises: *Adventure, Danger..."*

Jon hollers back. "What about the *Romance* part?"

The pilot chuckles and gives Jon a quick thumbs up. "You got some of that last time!"

Angie looks at Rollie questioningly. "What...?"

The pilot shrugs and replies, "One of Julio's cousins..." His reply has Angie thinking how most of Julio's relatives are excellent cooks. And, full-figured...

As Angie smiles to herself, Jon yells, "What...?"

Wrestling with the controls, Rollie calls back to Jon. "Relax... Sit back and take a nap. We'll be home in no time."

# Dominica Dash

Desperately clinging to the arm of his chair, Jon is jostled relentlessly, as the aircraft smashes through the turbulent skies. The forceful winds and the pounding rain make it nearly impossible to get any rest. Jon gazes out the starboard window for a moment, and then he turns his troubled stare forward.

# XXIX

Jon has his eyes closed, trying to calm himself and keep from vomiting. He focuses his mind on the hum of the engines and the sound of rain drumming on the metal skin of the aircraft. Suddenly, a voice rouses him from his meditation, and he opens his eyes to see Angie staring bewildered at him. "Jon…! Are you actually *sleeping?*"

Momentarily, he clenches his body, as the aircraft shudders violently. "Just preparing myself for the next challenging situation I've gotten myself into…"

"This would be the time to keep your peepers peeled. We're nearly home, but we're having a hard time maintaining radio contact. We can't pick up a location beacon."

Out the starboard window, all Jon can see are stormy skies and choppy waters. "What if we're blown off-course and miss Key West completely?"

Angie looks to Rollie, and then, with a smile, back at Jon. "We just don't want to end up in Cuba and have to eat dinner with Carlos."

Her mention of the Cuban businessman gives them both a good laugh, and then he turns back to the window. Through the haze, Jon sees a distant sliver of sunshine reflect off something ahead of them. He jumps out of his seat and points. "I think I see land to the north…"

Rollie pushes his headset microphone up and exclaims, "Damn, I sure hope so!" He leans over toward Angie to peek out her window and then banks the seaplane. At low altitude, they veer through the storm clouds toward the fleeting patch of sunlight. Engines roaring over choppy waters, they come upon the broken remains of the original overseas highway and then the Seven Mile Bridge. Rollie pumps his fist in the air and hollers back to his passenger. "Good eyes, Jon…! Now, we just follow the yellow-brick road."

~*~

On approach to Key West International Airport, the seaplane flies through the heavy rain to come in for a landing. Wheels extended, they taxi to the Fixed-Base Operator hangar, splashing down the tarmac through huge puddles and blown-in leafy debris. Once safely on the ground, Jon unbuckles his seatbelt and moves up to the cockpit. When he puts his hand on the pilot's seatback, his handcuffs dangle from one wrist. "Why didn't we put down at your seaplane base?"

Angie glances back. "We have to clear customs."

The pilot adds, "And, the water is way too rough to risk a water landing. The FBO will have tie downs to help the plane weather the storm."

Still feeling nauseous from the bumpy flight, Jon gulps. "When we were going to fly over open water, you said it was a *good* thing we were in a seaplane…"

Angie looks at Jon and stretches her arms upward. "Boys, I'm just happy to be back home."

The pilot pulls his headset off and looks back at Jon. "There's a big difference between having to put 'er down to rescue you and having to ditch in the ocean. If I'm over water, I'd rather be in a flying boat."

Jon looks outside, as the rain continues to pour down. "I'd rather be on dry land with a good roof over my head."

Angie pivots in her seat and gets up to chime in. "Hurricane season is when we find out if you're really made for life on the islands."

~*~

Inside the U.S. Customs office, Jon and Angie wait for Rollie to finish filing the appropriate paperwork. Finally, he strolls over and, with a smile, waves them along. "We're good to go. I'm gonna leave the plane here until the storm passes. More bad weather is heading this way. They're going to be shutting down the whole airport soon."

Angie watches the storm tracker on the television screen, as she stretches her back. "I have to get back to the tavern and make sure they batten-down the hatches."

Jon grabs his wet backpack and gets up to follow Angie. He stops in his tracks, suddenly realizing that he doesn't have the package given to him in Dominica. "I forgot something..."

Rollie and Angie turn to face him. The pilot asks, "Where...? In the plane?"

"No... Back there..."

Curious, Angie lifts an eyebrow. "I gathered everything you had with you at the hospital."

Rollie glances out the window to the thunderstorm. "We're *not* going back."

With a deep breath, Jon dolefully shakes his head. "Yeah, of course not... I, uh... It's just that I must have lost it on the boat ride."

Rollie turns and continues toward the door, and Angie waits for Jon. Concerned, she asks, "What was it you lost?"

He shakes his head to clear his fatigue and mutters, "Uh... It was nothing all that important."

She puts her arm over his shoulder and walks him toward the exit. "Having you back safe is what's important."

# XXX

They step outside the airport to torrents of rain. The small terminal looks like a ghost town. No attendants, taxi cabs, or rental cars in sight... Seeing no hint of a potential ride, Jon asks, "How are we going to get home?"

Rollie snorts, "I called us some transportation."

Jon, staring out into the storm, can barely see ten feet through the steady downpour. "If Ace brings the pickup truck, I guess I'll have to sit in the back?"

The pilot laughs. "We can do better than that."

A Key West Police Jeep rolls up and flashes its lights. As Jon curiously turns to look at Rollie, the pilot teasingly remarks, "You'll be riding in the back of this one."

Angie snickers at the sight of the emergency lights and picks up her travel bag. "Nice to see our tax dollars at work."

# Dominica Dash

The window rolls down, and Detective Lyle peers out at them through the rain. "I don't think this weather is going to let up for some time. Get in."

As Rollie opens the door, Angie yells to him, "Shotgun! I call riding shotgun." Rollie rolls his eyes and holds the door open for her to get in. Swinging it closed behind her, he quickly climbs into the back of the Jeep.

When Jon follows, the loose end of his handcuffs hits the door frame. The distinct sound causes Detective Lyle to peer over his shoulder. He shakes his head, as he notices the cuffs and takes in the rest of Jon's odd attire. "Nice outfit, Springer. *You be jammin'?* Heck, I won't even ask where they came from."

Rollie pipes in. "Souvenir from the tropics…"

Settled in the backseat with Rollie, Jon holds his wet backpack on his lap. Up front, Angie wipes some fog from the window, and Detective Lyle looks over at her. "Where to…?"

The pilot leans forward to the wire cage separating the front from the back. "The seaplane base, please…"

Lyle glances back at him. "I'm only making one stop, pal. This isn't a shuttle service."

Angie smiles at the detective. "My car is there."

The detective shifts into gear, and the Jeep splashes forward through the downpour. "Fine… Rollie's place it is." The police vehicle flashes its emergency lights, as it leaves the nearly vacant airport.

~*~

They arrive at the seaplane base under a dark sky flickering with occasional bursts of lightning. The Jeep pulls through the gate and drives up to a hangar with

145

lights glowing inside. As Detective Lyle parks, the rain shimmers in the orange glow of outdoor flood lamps.

Ace appears just inside the big doors and looks out to see who has arrived. First, he sees Angie step out and dash to the cover of the hangar. He looks at her and asks, "You alone?" When Rollie climbs out next, he crinkles his brow and adds, "Heck, I could've picked the two of you up."

They watch, as Rollie exchanges a few words with Lyle. Then, Ace mutters, "Is the water-bird nested at the airport?"

She nods. "Yes... We had to clear customs, and he didn't want to risk a water landing in this weather."

The mechanic looks out to the dark, churning waters. "Doing military rescues in my day, we landed in worse... But, with this storm coming in, it's probably good to have it tied down on higher ground."

Rollie trots over to them through the downpour and gives Ace a smile. "Good to see you, pal."

"Everything okay...?"

"You know...The usual..."

The mechanic gestures to the police vehicle idling with its back door open. "Why's he sticking around?"

Rollie ducks inside the hangar door to get out of the rain. "We picked up a friend on the way."

Ace looks from Rollie to Angie, and back again. "Jon...?"

She laughs. "He had a little trouble with the locals."

Amused, the mechanic shakes his head. "Kinda figures. That fella finds more trouble than most."

Inside the Jeep, Jon scoots over to get out, and Lyle holds up a hand. "Hold it a second, Springer. Anything to say?"

"Uh, thanks for the ride?"

The detective pivots to look at the cuffs dangling from Jon's wrist. "How are you going to get those off?"

"I haven't really thought about it. Maybe, order a key on the internet…?"

Lyle grimaces, reaches into his cup holder and pulls out a tiny handcuff key. "Try this, smart-ass." Jon fits the key into the cuffs, turns it and the shackle releases.

"Thank you…" He offers to return the key, but the detective waves him off.

"Keep it. No use having a pair of handcuffs, if you can't get them off."

"I don't plan on using them again."

"Ya *never know…*"

"Uh, okay…? Thanks, I guess."

As Jon slips out of the vehicle, Detective Lyle warns, "The *big* storm will be right on us by morning. Keep your head down, and don't do anything stupid like flying a kite or tying yourself to a lamp post. The place you stay at has a storm cellar under the main house. If you need to, use it."

With his bag in hand, Jon nods and steps out. "See ya."

Looking in the rearview mirror, the detective watches him exit. "Not if I see you first."

# XXXI

Swinging the car door closed, Jon steps back as the police Jeep drives forward, pulls around to make the turn out of the lot, and drives off. Jon trots through the downpour to join the others in the hangar.

Glad to be out of the weather, he tucks the handcuffs into the pocket of his baggy pants. Ace looks him over and smirks. "Gone native, have ya?"

Wringing some of the water from his outfit, Jon grins. "Just trying to blend in."

Rollie sweeps wet hair from his face and looks to Angie. "Ya sure ya don't want to stay here until the storm passes?"

"I should get back to the Conch and make sure things are in order."

He looks to Jon. "How about you?"

# Dominica Dash

"I just want to change into dry clothes, brush my teeth and crawl into bed for a few days."

Angie pats his arm and smiles at his comical outfit. "C'mon… I'll give you a ride home."

Ace waves, as he wanders toward the hangar office. "Okay, see y'all later."

Rollie stands by the large doorway, ready to close it after the two are outside. "I'll make sure things are in order here and catch up with both of you later."

Angie reaches a hand up and casually touches the seaplane pilot's whiskered cheek before giving a sultry wink. "Yeah… See ya later, Rollie."

With their bags, Angie and Jon dart out through the pouring rain to a small Mazda sports car. Jon looks at the sporty two-seater and smiles. "Nice car you have here."

She pats the convertible and pulls the door open. "It's a lot more fun on *sunny* days." Jon slides in on the passenger side, and the engine starts like it's ready to race.

As the rain hammers down, the sports car backs around, shifts gears and rolls out of the parking lot.

~*~

Splashing through flooded streets, the small car makes its way across the island of Key West. At Jon's home, she pulls up to the side gate and stops at the water-filled curb. She shifts the car to neutral and looks over at her drenched passenger. "How are you holding together?"

"I don't think I ever want to be on a boat again."

"How about airplanes…?"

"Big or small…?"

149

She raises an eyebrow and laughs. "Lots of adventures were had on *this* trip, eh?"

"I might need a break from flying, too."

"Unless you have a problem with my driving, it's the only other way off this island."

"I guess I'll have to stick around, then."

Sweeping her hand over the dash to wipe away the dust, Angie comments, "The worst of this storm is supposed to make landfall tomorrow. I'll keep the bar open for anyone who wants to have a hurricane party."

"Hurricane party...?"

"On the islands, sunshine and bad weather are just two sides of the same coin. Some choose to pray for their safety and for the storm to pass, while others raise a glass to toast Mother Nature and all her fury."

Jon stares at the windshield wipers, as they try, in vain, to fight off the downpour. As if in a trance, he thinks aloud. "Yeah... I guess there's a lot of ways to face your fears."

"Owning a tavern, I'm in the *party-till-it's-over* group."

He smiles at her and lifts the wet backpack from his lap. "I'm gonna throw everything in the dryer and crawl into bed."

"Do it before the power goes out."

"The electricity...?"

"The storm is bound to knock down a few power lines, and it could be out for days."

"Okay... I didn't think about that."

"I have a backup generator at the bar, and a lot of other places do, too, so it won't be that bad."

# Dominica Dash

Angie reaches over and lays her hand on Jon's arm. "Things *can* get rough sometimes, but, if you make it through, someday, they'll be great stories to tell."

"Okay… Thanks."

As the rain continues to pour down, Jon opens the passenger door to get out, and Angie reaches over to stop him. "Oh, and congratulations on your book!"

"Thanks. We'll see how it does."

"If you wrote your best, it will do fine."

"They say a new book has the shelf life of yogurt, so we'll see." He gets out, as she laughs and waves.

In the rain, Jon swings the door closed and hops over the rivulet of water at the curb. He stands watching, as Angie's car shifts into gear and drives down the palm-lined street. Shrugging-off the downpour, he hitches his bag over his shoulder, turns and passes through the side yard gate.

# XXXII

Jon steps inside the garage apartment and flips on the lights. Looking over to his laptop computer sitting on the table where he left it, he momentarily considers writing. While scanning his apartment and its décor, Jon is hit with a rush of *déjà vu* and the strange feeling that everything that just happened could have been a dream.

He looks down at his soaking-wet backpack, drops it to the floor and shakes his head. "If it *was* a dream, it was definitely a very traumatic one…" He pulls the handcuffs from his pocket and places them on the table next to his computer.

Still sporting the Jamaica t-shirt and MC Hammer pants, he cruises through the kitchen, grabs a bottle of beer from the refrigerator and goes to sit on the couch. After taking a drink, he sets the bottle down on the coffee table, lays his head back, and is asleep straightaway.

# Dominica Dash

~*~

The storm blows sheets of rain against the windows and bends the trees on the property nearly to the breaking point. Oblivious to it all, Jon lays, passed-out, on the couch, until the phone rings and jolts him awake. He reaches over to lift the receiver from the cradle. "Hello...?"

The tone of his agent's piercing voice shoots right through him. "Hey, Johnny Boy...! Where you at?"

Dazed, Jon sits up, pauses, and looks around the room. He sees the storm raging outside and remembers where he is. "I'm in my Key West apartment. That's where you called me."

Moselly laughs. "I hardly ever know *where*, let alone *who*, I'm calling. My secretary keeps the calendar and the rolodex, and she puts me through to whomever."

"That's okay... I'll get the number changed."

Not really listening, Moselly continues. "That's great, but you're supposed to be headed to Mexico City for your new book's launch party tonight."

"I don't think I'm going to make it."

"Horsepucky... I'm sending a private jet for you."

Jon rubs sleep from his eyes and looks outside. "No good... The airport is probably shut down by now."

"Who would shut down an airport?"

"Hurricane Anita..."

"Who's that?"

"Turn on the weather channel."

The literary agent clicks on his television, sees that the Caribbean is under a storm-watch and groans. "Well, damn.... That blows..."

"Yeah, that's exactly why they shut it down."

"What…?"

Jon sighs, "Why are you calling me, Moselly?"

"I'm about to go to the airport and get myself on a private jet that's headed to your premiere."

"Have fun."

"Ya *sure* you're not coming?"

The windows rattle, as the wind blows harder. "Yeah, pretty sure… The storm is really coming in."

"I don't know why you'd want to stay in a place with hurricanes or tornados or whatever they have there."

Jon snorts, "Earthquakes don't bother you?"

"Not really… A few seconds of the earth moving just shakes things up and keeps it interesting."

"Have fun at the book premiere."

"*Everyone* will be having a good time. Except *you*… Oh, and by the way, your other book sold a few copies."

Pleasantly surprised, Jon beams. "Oh, yeah…? That's great."

"Not really… Didn't you hear me? I said a *few* copies. Your adventure books sell a *lot* of copies!"

"Send me a check."

"If this one sells like the others, I'll send you a *car*."

"Okay, just not a boat."

"What I'm gonna do, first thing next week, is send you a cell phone, so I can find you whenever I need to."

"Don't bother."

On the other end of the line, Jon hears a door slam and girls giggling. Moselly shushes them and returns to the call. "You're gonna miss out on a really fun time!"

"Sounds like you're already starting."

"Even without you, the party must go on."

"Talk to ya later, Moselly."

"I'll send you that cell phone."

"Please don't."

"Ciao, baby…!"

The connection clicks off and Jon hangs up the phone. He looks at the rotary dial, then lifts the handset again and sets it beside the base, keeping the line off the hook and preventing any more unexpected calls. Noticing his beverage sitting on the coffee table, he is tempted to take another swig. He looks at his watch, and sees that he has slept through most of the night. "Breakfast of champions…"

Jon lays back down on the couch and turns to look out the window. The hurricane shows no sign of letting up, in fact, it seems to have worsened. Exhausted, Jon closes his eyes, takes a deep breath and quickly falls back to sleep.

~*~

At the Key West Air Charters base, heavy gusts of wind blow the rain sideways, raking across the hangar's metal doors. Two figures dash outside and get into the old truck in front. The engine cranks a few times, catches, and then finally starts. Idling, the truck rolls backward a few feet, shifts into gear, and drives out of the fenced lot.

# XXXIII

Asleep on the couch, Jon is oblivious to the hurricane force winds blowing outside. Suddenly, Jon bolts upright, as a loud pounding on the screen door shakes him from his slumber. To his surprise, the front door opens, and Rollie, soaking wet, stands in the entryway. "Hey, pal… You awake?"

"Kinda…"

"I would have called first, but your phone is out."

Jon looks at his old-fashioned telephone and hangs up the receiver. "I was trying to get some sleep."

"Let's go."

"Where…?"

"The *real* storm is finally here and we're all going to the Conch Tavern for a hurricane party."

"Why?"

"Safest place in town…!"

"Really…?"

The pilot smirks. "I don't know, but they're well-stocked with booze and grub. *Everyone* is going."

Slowly waking up, Jon looks down at his comical outfit. "Actually, I should grab a shower and clean up a bit first."

"Heck, you'll get a wet-down on the way to the truck. It's really dumping good out there. I'm glad I have a seaplane, 'cause Noah would be building an arc about now!"

With a complacent shrug, Jon gets up and looks at his damp backpack still by the doorway. "I didn't even unpack any of my wet things."

Rollie steps inside and away from the splash of the rain. "If you have anything left after the storm washes the island, you can worry about it then."

Jon looks around the room. "Should we be evacuating?"

"Too late for that…"

Now awake and grasping the situation, Jon stammers, "But, people can *die* in hurricanes."

"With your crazy luck, you'll have a brush with death and come out smelling like a rose. Who knows, maybe someone will choke on a handful of mixed nuts at the Conch."

Determined to let go of his anxiety, Jon takes a breath. "If I've survived everything else that's happened in Key West, I guess an old-fashioned hurricane is naturally the next thing."

Rollie pats Jon on the back, as they head out the door. "*That's* the attitude… Life is *full* of unpleasant adventures." Following that bit of guidance, they step into the pouring rain, dash down the stairway, and head out through the garden gate to Rollie's truck parked at the curb.

The street's gutter surges with running water, and the idling truck, with Ace at the wheel, sits just beyond the flow. Jon opens the passenger door and slides in, followed by Rollie. The driver looks at Jon and grins. "Ahoy there... You sure do like them awful duds."

Jon pushes his wet hair back and situates himself in the middle of the small bench seat. "They're comfortable."

As Rollie pulls the heavy door shut, he points a finger over the dashboard. "Onward to the Conch Republic Tavern!" Ace shifts the truck into gear, hits the gas, and drives down the flooded street. The windshield wipers whip back and forth, effective for only a second at a time, as splashes of water peel off to the side.

Jon gazes through the windows at the rain-filled streets. "Dang... Is it safe to drive with the roads flooded like this?"

Rollie laughs and scoots over, so that water dripping from the loose seal around the door won't get his pants wetter. "Sure... It's just a Splash-In."

Knowingly, Ace peers past Jon to the seaplane pilot. "Safer with me driving than him... That nut would be doing touch-'n-goes along the curbs. Or, pulling someone down Duval Street in a rental kayak."

Jon looks at Rollie. "Sounds like there's a story..."

The pilot grins guiltily. "Sure, but it was just that one time, and no one got seriously hurt."

# Dominica Dash

"What happened?"

Ace grunts, "On a sharp turn, the kayak slipped up a curb's handicap ramp and launched through the plate glass window of a store."

Defensively, Rollie offers, "It didn't hurt the kayak, and they were looking to remodel anyway."

With a reluctant chuckle, the gruff mechanic adds, "Luckily, they had storm insurance, and claimed it was a bunch of *rogue coconuts*."

Laughing, Jon relaxes in the seat, trying to enjoy the ride.

# XXXIV

The garden area outside the Conch Republic Tavern is a flooded mess of broken palm fronds and other leafy debris. After parking on the street, Ace scoots from the truck and darts toward the entrance. In a moment, Jon and Rollie follow.

Seeing a trinket-decorated bicycle parked against a tree, in a puddle of water, Jon comments, "Hey, even Aston is here!"

Rollie scoots past him and grabs the handle to the door. "It's not safe to be out where his raft-shack is buoyed, and, in here, it's a *who's who* of the island, when a storm comes to visit." He pulls the door open to see Ace, just inside, along with the sound of people having a good time. "Like a family reunion, where everyone gets along fine, until the sun comes out or the liquor runs dry."

# Eric H. Heisner

As the hurricane continues to churn in the sky, the torrential rain pelts them at the doorway. They slip into the shelter of the tavern, and the heavy door closes behind them. Following Rollie's lead, Jon steps into the crowded barroom. He notices a lot of familiar faces, from Aston to local regulars. Even Detective Lyle… They make their way to the bar, as Angie starts to pour a Sunset Ale. She turns from the tapper to look them over and smiles sweetly. "Hey, Jon… Looks like you didn't waste any time cleaning up."

A little embarrassed, he looks down at his soaking wet t-shirt and baggy pants. "I didn't know how to dress for a Hurricane Party."

She places a perfectly poured glass of ale in front of Jon. "*Every* day is a party in Key West, and you're not dressed any stranger than some in here." Just as she finishes her sentence, Aston comes up behind them, outfitted in his eccentric, islander attire and holding a pirate-style tin cup.

"Hey dere, writer-mon!"

Jon lifts his beer, takes a sip and pivots to greet the island sage. "Hey, Aston. Nice to see you."

He looks Jon over, tilts his head and grins approvingly. "I be likin' yer new wardrobe style."

Jon nods self-consciously. "It's on loan. *Sort of…*"

Angie chimes in. "*Permanent* loan, you could say."

Raising an eyebrow, Aston lowers his voice so that only the small group can hear. "I hear ya done da *Dominica Dash* and only have da stories ta show for it."

# Dominica Dash

Nearly choking on a swallow of beer, Jon looks at Rollie, and then Angie, with surprise. "News gets around fast."

The pilot holds up his hands in protest. "I didn't say anything."

Angie shakes her head. "Me, neither…"

A shapely woman, dressed to the nines, slips from the crowd and enters the conversation. "I might have let it slip."

Jon and Rollie turn to see Giselle and can hardly take their eyes off her gorgeous figure. Rollie catches a glare from Angie and diverts his eyes from the ample cleavage.

Angie wipes away a puddle on the bar and groans, "Look what blew in…"

Jon stutters, "Uh, hello…"

Rollie exclaims, "You look *fantast*… Uh, you look nice." He puts an elbow to the bar and leans in toward the bar owner. "I'll have a rum punch."

"You'll end up with a double *Conch-Punch-in-the-Kisser,* if you're not *careful*."

From the fringe of the group, Ace slides in, puts his hand on the bar and mutters, "I'll just have a regular ol' beer, thanks."

Giselle shimmies up next to Jon and whispers, "I'm sorry for what you had to go through to get that painting."

Surprised, Jon utters, "How did you know about *that?*"

"Key West is a small town. When special favors need to be called in, there are only a few places to go and get them."

Jon sips his drink and nervously smiles at the owner of the Clipped Kitty. "I guess you know or are, at least, good friends with Jeanee' Renee'?"

"I have many friends."

"Thank you for whatever you did to get me out of there."

She gives him a sultry smile. "Thank you for the effort."

Jon shakes his head. "I didn't accomplish anything. Basically, I got into a mess and then tried my best to get out." Giselle places a slender hand on his arm to comfort him, sending a warm shiver through his body.

A bit jealous, Angie taps the bar to get some attention. "Hey, Jon... Do you need anything to eat or drink, before we make your announcement?"

Jon looks at the woman on his arm and then to his beer. Curious, he tilts his head and asks, "What announcement?"

Suddenly, Jon gets a sharp jab in his side and turns to see Casey Kettles glaring at him over yellow sunglasses. "Hey you, Hollywood-schmoozer... Stop groping my mom!"

Embarrassed, Jon immediately steps back from Giselle and looks at the snarky teenager. "Uh, I wasn't..."

Casey pushes his sunshades up on his nose and laughs. "Just *kidding*, dummy! This hurricane will probably kill us all, so ya better get one good smooch in while you can."

# Dominica Dash

Jon turns back to Giselle and smiles good-humoredly. Interrupted by the clanking of a ship's bell, everyone turns to watch Angie give it another ring, before she addresses the crowd. *"Can I have everyone's attention...?!"*

# XXXV

$A$s everyone turns to the woman behind the bar, the chatter dies down. Angie steps up on a wooden crate and announces, "Thank y'all for coming. It's a rager outside, but that doesn't prevent us from living our lives." She looks over the crowd, seeing many familiar faces. "Speaking of livin' the good life, one of our newest friends here in the Florida Keys has finished a feat that takes a good measure of patience and perseverance." Angie waves her arm toward Jon, and everyone turns to where he stands, completely dumbfounded, with a beer in his hand. She continues, "Jon Springer came to the Keys to find his muse. In the spirit of writers who have graced our island paradise, like Hemingway, Blume, and Buffett, he has opened himself up to life and newfound adventures, finding that a life well-lived is a life worth writing about."

She smiles at Jon, and he looks at all the friendly faces gathered in the room "Thank you..."

# Dominica Dash

"It is with my great pleasure that I present to you all, Jon's first bit of novel writing…"

On cue, the door of the tavern opens and Carlos, wet from the rain, steps in. Dressed in his classic Cuban-elite attire, he holds two hardcover copies of Jon's new book and waves them overhead, as a sports champion or car salesman might. Behind him, Jorge carries two medium-sized cardboard boxes.

The ship's bell clanks again, and Angie announces to all, "Our Cuban pal, Carlos Murietta, has generously purchased one hundred copies of Jon's new book to give anyone in this room who can actually read."

Rollie hollers above the din. "He'll probably have to donate about ninety-five percent of them to libraries in Cuba!" The crowd erupts in drunken cheers and laughter. Angie clanks the bell a few more times to settle everyone down, as Carlos makes his way to the bar.

Angie waves Jon over. "If Jon would be so kind as to autograph a few, that would make this hurricane party slash book launch event a success!" When she lifts a glass for a toast, everyone else in the room lifts theirs. "Cheers to *life well-lived!*"

"CHEERS!!!"

Carlos walks over to Jon with his books and produces a fancy fountain pen from his shirt pocket. "Mister Springer, could I have the honor of getting the very first autograph?"

Jon sets his beer down and takes the pen and book offered by the Cuban. "Thank you, Carlos…" He scribbles a message on the title page and hands the book and pen back. Carlos flashes his Cheshire grin and only takes the book.

"Keep the pen. A present... You'll be needing it tonight." He hands the other book to Jon. "Could I have just an autograph in this one?" Jon looks at him questioningly, and the Cuban's grin gets wider. He adds, "Perhaps if I was to sell it."

Behind them, Jorge opens one of the boxes and starts to hand out books to the crowd. A line forms, and Jon begins signing copies of his novel. Carlos leans over and suggests, "After the storm, if my boat isn't at the bottom of the marina, we should invite Angie along with us for a sunset cruise."

Jon turns to him and shakes his head. "I think I'm done venturing out on the water for a bit."

The Cuban looks mildly offended. "You cannot blame Mother Nature for doing what she is meant to do. We are mere passengers on her heaving breast."

Drink in hand, Rollie leans toward them and interjects. "We had some rough weather flying in yesterday, and he had a heck of a boat ride before that."

Carlos shrugs and turns his gaze to Angie. "My dear... How is it you gringos say...? You *must* get back on the horse."

Giselle slips closer and propositions Jon. "Maybe you'd like to come over to my place and get on one of mine?"

Rollie audibly gulps and glances toward Angie, who watches disapprovingly. To Jon, he casually remarks, "If you want smooth sailing, she has one of the nicest ones around." Angie stares wide-eyed at Rollie, and he stutters innocently. "Sailboats... I'm talking about her twin-masted sailboat!"

Jon continues to autograph books. Surprisingly, the next person in line is Casey. Jon takes the book to sign, and, before he can say anything nice, the teenager offers a snide comment. "Yes, I *can* read..."

Jon glances at his wristwatch to check that it hasn't been lifted by the troublesome youth. "I'm just shocked that you didn't *steal* it."

Timidly, Casey pulls another book from under his shirt and hands it to Jon. "Could you put a signature on this one, too? For a friend of mine..."

Jon finishes with the first, hands it back and then signs the pilfered copy. "I hope you enjoy it."

The teen smirks. "I hope it has lots of sexy adventures, like those J. T. Springs novels Rollie reads."

Jon glances over at the pilot, who shrugs in defense. "Sometimes I take old copies over to the Clipped Kitty for the girls to read."

Finished signing, Jon turns back to Casey. "Probably not, but there might be some similarities in writing style. This story could be a *bit* more highbrow."

Disappointed, Casey looks at his books and considers handing one of them back. "Then again, maybe my friend won't enjoy it."

Rollie pipes in. "That reminds me, there's a new *Springs* adventure book just out. I think it takes place in the Yucatan. I'll have to send a copy to my pal, Julio, since it looks to be his neck of the woods. Wonder if he did any consulting work?"

# Eric H. Heisner

Feeling guilty about his secret alias, Jon looks at Rollie. "I wouldn't be surprised. Writers write about what they know."

The seaplane pilot slaps Jon on the back and laughs. "Yeah, Springer... That's why we have to keep *you* out on the trail of *adventure!* We don't want to read about some guy who sits on his ass in a garage apartment."

Jon goes back to signing books. As the hurricane rages, the party carries on into the late hours of the night.

# XXXVI

As a new day breaks, the gale-force winds continue to blow. The rain has mostly stopped, and the cloudy skies don't seem to have the dark ferociousness they had during days prior. Streets are flooded and debris is everywhere. A few people are outside inspecting property damage.

Inside the tavern, the music, at a much lower volume, still plays. The lights are dimmed, which gives little indication to the actual time of day. Some people curl up on the floor with blankets, while others sleep with their heads down on the bar.

Jon is hanging out with Rollie and Ace at a table toward the back of the room. Nearly asleep, the mechanic, with his feet up on another seat leans his chair back. As people fade-off or quietly drift outside, Jon looks around the room. "I haven't been out this late... Or, *early*, in a long time."

Rollie takes a sip of his mixed drink and nods his head. "I can't usually afford to tie one on like this, in case I have to fly somewhere or jump into the ring."

"How's the boxing going?"

"I win about as much as I lose."

Jon thinks about the pain of his own recent beating. "When do you think you'll retire?"

"Retire...? Why? I enjoy it, and, in a few years, I can join the senior division and beat up on old guys."

Snorting himself awake in his chair, Ace is confused. "Wha... What? You talkin' 'bout me?"

Jon and Rollie share a laugh, and then the pilot responds. "Hush... Go back to sleep, old man. Nobody's flying today..."

Angie comes from the back room with a bottle of coffee liqueur. Stepping over sleeping bodies, she struts to their table. "Good news... Saw the weather report, and it looks like the worst of the storm has passed. It's moving out over the Gulf."

"Wonder how my plane fared..."

She looks to Rollie. "I called the airport, and they said there is minimal damage overall. Just a lot of cleanup to do. Planes are all in order, and the terminal should open today."

A person rouses from their sleep and wanders outside. When the door opens, Jon catches a glimpse of cloudy skies. "Looks like there is a lot more to hurricane cleanup than just sweeping the streets."

# Dominica Dash

Angie pulls up a chair, sets the bottle on the table and looks at the remaining customers scattered around the room. "They're good folks. Like family... One night together is fine, but, after that, you start to wear on each other." She gives a chuckle. "This is the only time I let anyone sleep in the bar. Usually, if you start to wink out, I say *hit the road, Go home*."

She gathers up three glasses and cracks the bottle open. Jon shakes his head. "None for me, thanks."

Angie turns to him with a persuasive smile. "Nonsense... It's a special occasion to have your first book released. Besides, I bought this bottle when Carlos and I were in Mexico rescuing you and Rollie."

The pilot smirks. "I'll drink to *that!*"

Jon tilts his tired head. "It's kinda late for a nightcap."

She pours them each a drink and passes them around. "Then, how about we call it breakfast?"

Rollie raises his glass. "Cheers to surviving yet another one of life's unexpected storms."

Taking the drink offered him, Jon sighs. "Seems I've had a few of those since moving here."

Angie lifts her glass for another toast. "We're not livin' this life for a long time, so it might as well be for a good time."

They clink their glasses together and drink. Jon lets the liqueur settle and takes a breath. "*Mmm*, that's good..."

Angie grins. "Carlos is a big pain in the you-know-what, but he knows where to go to get the good stuff."

Jon looks around the room. "Where is he?"

"He offered to let me to stay at his apartment. For *safety*... I declined, so he retired early."

Rollie grunts, "Safe from the storm, but not the grope." She gives the pilot a knowing look and turns to watch Jon fiddle with his glass and take another sip.

Jon looks back at her. "That was really nice of you to have Carlos pick up a few of my books."

She nods. "That's what friends are for."

"I hope people enjoy it."

With a nonchalant shrug, she offers, "What's it matter?

Jon holds his glass and looks around. "Working alone all the time, you never know what people think."

Angie replies, "You created a story the best you could. Some will like it, and some won't. Doesn't reflect how hard you worked at it."

Rollie pours another drink. "The same with my flying... You go out and do your job the best you can with what the world throws at you. Sometimes I get generous tips and smiles, and sometimes I have to clean-up vomit."

Lifting an eyebrow, Angie eyes Rollie. "Well, you're quite the flying philosopher. Maybe Jon can teach you to write a book on it someday?"

"It would be a very short story. I'll leave the creative stuff to the professionals. I'm just here to rescue him, when he gets too deep into his research." They laugh, thinking of their latest escapade.

When someone opens the door, they see that the wind has stopped, and a bit of sunshine is breaking through the clouds. Jon finishes his drink, pushes his chair back and stands. He looks down at his comical outfit and tries to brush a stain from his shirt. "I'm gonna go home and slip into something... *Something else.*"

Rollie raises his glass and takes a sip. "See ya, buddy."

Sweetly, Angie adds, "Good job on the finished book. What's the plan for the next one?"

"Just ideas so far..."

She laughs. "At least you have ideas to write."

As Jon walks to the door, Ace snorts himself awake again and looks around the quiet barroom. In a daze, he asks, "Did someone say breakfast?"

Angie pours a drink for Ace and slides him the glass. "Here ya go, ol' timer." After putting the cork back in the bottle, Angie glances across the table and gives Rollie a sultry look. "*I'm* gonna slip into something more comfortable, *too.*"

"Need any help?"

"Not if you have to fly off later..."

Pretending to look at the time on his watch, Rollie shakes his head. "Nope... My schedule is clear for the next few days."

She smiles. "I guess hurricanes aren't *all* bad."

Jon opens the door to see the storm's damage and glances back, as Angie and Rollie are getting up from the table. Too tired to think anything about it, he steps outside.

# XXXVII

While walking home, Jon gazes around at the mess of broken trees and debris. A few cars splash past him, as he jumps over an overflowing storm gutter and strolls down the block toward the gated yard of the estate. Climbing over a downed tree in order to access the side entrance, Jon makes his way through the garden and heads toward the garage apartment in back.

Stepping into the apartment to the ring of his telephone, Jon moves across the room to answer it. "Hello... Jon here."

"Oh, ho, ho Johnny boy...! How in the heck are ya! You missed one helluva bang-up premiere last night!"

"I had myself a pretty good time here."

Not really listening, the agent on the phone continues. "I've never seen anything like it! A storm blew

177

# Eric H. Heisner

in, and the floral blouses of the señoritas turned into a wild, wet t-shirt contest. The Mariachis got drunk, let a jaguar loose and tried to rope it. And, somehow, I lost all my clothes except for a sombrero!"

"Sounds like a fun book launch."

"One of your best! When do I get another one?"

Jon cradles the receiver on his shoulder and looks across the room at a new piece of framed artwork hung over the couch. A small envelope is tucked behind the corner of it, so Jon walks over to inspect. "I don't know... I'm working on a few things."

"Well, your last one will be another huge success, judging from the party."

Jon stands staring at the mystery painting. He mutters, "Is that a good way to gauge a book?"

"You're not gonna give me another *Jonathan Springer* novella, are you? I think it only pre-sold a hundred copies... Give me a good *J. T. Springs* story! With sex, adventure, and whatever else kinda good stuff you put in there..."

Jon slips the envelope from behind the artwork and sees that it has his name on it. "I'll come up with something."

"Great...! Send me the pages. Now, I need to find myself some new duds before my flight home. I don't think they'll let me back in the country with just a sombrero and a smile."

"Bye, Moselly..."

"Ciao, baby...!"

Jon hangs up the phone and takes the note from the envelope. It reads:

# Dominica Dash

Dear *Jonathan*,

*I am sorry about the hassle in Dominica. Usually, the process is much easier, but with the present political climate, things have become difficult. I trust that you made it home safely, and I look forward to making your acquaintance at some future date.*

*Sincerely,*
*Jeanee' Renee'*

Jon tucks the note back into the envelope and looks at the painting. After staring at it for a while, he wipes the drowsiness from his eyes. "I was interrogated, beaten-up, chased through the jungle, almost drowned in a small boat and flew through a hurricane… For *that…?* I guess art *is* subjective." Jon tosses the envelope on the coffee table near his wet backpack and heads down the hallway to go to bed.

~*~

The following day, with the sun shining, Key West looks like it appears on postcards. A tropical paradise… Down the street from Jon's place, Rollie's truck comes around the corner, swerves around the downed tree and parks along the curb. Rollie makes his way through the garden gate, heads up to the garage apartment and raps his knuckles on the screen door. "Hey Jon… Rise and shine!"

Jon pushes the door open and steps aside to let him in. "Hey Rollie, what's up?"

Rollie notices that Jon is dressed in his usual outfit of short-sleeved button-down shirt and shorts. He looks over at the computer on the table and asks, "Doing some writing?"

"Some… I'm probably finished for the day."

"Good… Put on your boating shoes and come with me for the day."

"To where…?

"A sailboat ride…!"

Jon shakes his head. "No, thanks. I'd like to give it a few more days at least for the memory of nearly drowning to fade."

"Nonsense…! You don't want to miss *this* cruise."

Reluctantly, Jon gets his shoes and then sits on a chair to put them on. He looks at Rollie. "Whose boat?"

"That's a surprise. We have a special invitation that you *don't* want to pass up."

"Who will be there?"

"A bunch of important people, along with me and you… Carlos might even be there." Rollie glances out the doorway. "Oh, and don't mention anything to Angie, if you can help it. She bristles at the strangest things."

Finishing with his shoes, Jon looks at him suspiciously. "I'm not going to end up in jail somewhere, am I?"

"Why would you say that?"

Jon passes the table and closes the screen of his laptop. He looks at the set of handcuffs next to the computer and sighs. "With good reason…"

They are about to leave the apartment, when Rollie suddenly stops to stare at the artwork hanging over the couch. "Where did you get that painting?"

Jon turns and looks at it. "Long story…"

# Dominica Dash

"It's fantastic. I love it!"

Taking another look, Jon tilts his head to see if he's missing something. Finally, they head down the steps and out to Rollie's truck, as the screen door slams behind them.

# XXXVIII

A twin-masted sailing vessel cuts through aqua-blue waters. The high-end yacht is operated by a neatly uniformed crew, and a special waitstaff serves food and cocktails on the deck. The Caribbean view is outstanding, only matched by the level of service to the guests.

Jon stands with Rollie amongst a crowd of wealthy men, some with their much-younger wives or, possibly, girlfriends. He turns to his pilot friend and grins. "Wow, this is pretty nice. I guess this is how the other half lives."

"I *told* you it was not to be missed."

Jon raises his cocktail glass to Carlos, across the deck, entertaining a small group of women. The Cuban grins back and lifts his own cocktail in return. Jon leans over to Rollie. "So… who is the *owner* of this boat?"

# Dominica Dash

Scanning the faces in the crowd, Rollie replies, "She is a certain charismatic somebody who uses it for mostly business. To entertain some of her more important clients..."

Jon's first thought is that of his mysterious landlord. "You've *met* Jeanee' Renee'?"

Rollie has a sip of his fancy drink and shakes his head. "No, but I've heard *stories* about her. Why?"

"Does *she* own this boat?"

The seaplane pilot looks past Jon, grins, and lifts his drink in a saluting gesture. Jon hears a familiar voice behind him, and, when he turns, he comes face-to-face with Giselle. "Hello, Mister Springer. I am so honored that you could be my special guest."

Dumbfounded by Giselle's presence, Jon stammers. "Uh, hello again... *This* is *yours?*"

Her eyes sparkle, as she offers him a seductive smile. "Well, I thought it was important to have you out for a jaunt on the ocean without requiring you to risk life and limb."

Feeling his whole-body flush with delight, Jon nods. "That would certainly be a welcome experience."

She slides an arm under his and gives Rollie a sly wink. "If I can steal you away from your pilot-friend, I'll introduce you to some important people." Rollie smiles and has another swallow of his drink, as she continues. "See you later, Rollie."

With a nod, he grins back. "Giselle..."

The attractive host leads Jon away through the distinguished crowd. Overhead, the crisp, white sails

# Eric H. Heisner

snap in the wind, as the magnificent ship glides across the blue ocean waters and into the sunset.

The End...

If you enjoyed **Conch Republic vol. IV**,
read other stories by
*Eric H. Heisner*
www.leandogproductions.com

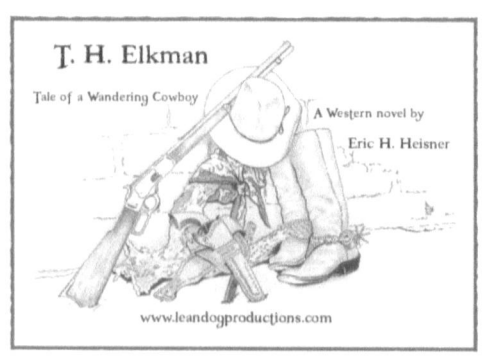

T. H. Elkman

Tale of a Wandering Cowboy

A Western novel by

Eric H. Heisner

www.leandogproductions.com

WEST TO BRAVO

A Western Novel

By Eric H. Heisner

WWW.LEANDOGPRODUCTIONS.COM

Wings of the Pirate

A high-flying Adventure Novel

By Eric H. Heisner

Limited time pre-order at:

www.inkshares.com

illustrations by

Al P. Bringas

www.leandogproductions.com

**Eric H. Heisner** is an award-winning writer, actor and filmmaker. He is the author of several Western and Adventure novels: *West to Bravo, T. H. Elkman, Africa Tusk, Conch Republic* and *Short Western Tales: Friend of the Devil*. He can be contacted at his website:

www.leandogproductions.com

Emily Jean Mitchell is an artist, teacher, and mother who enjoys spending time in the garden and outdoor laytime with her husband, children and dog in Austin, Texas.

www.mlemitchellart.com